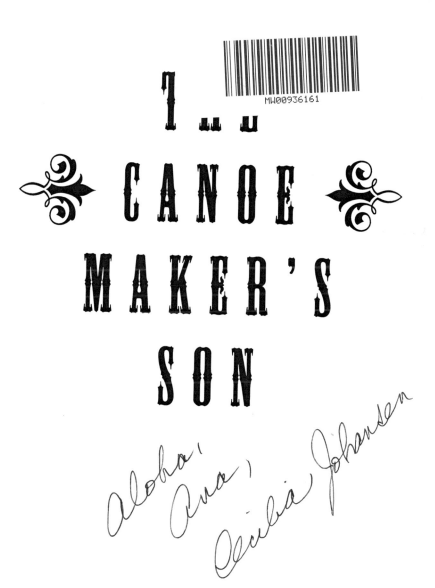

THE
CANOE
MAKER'S
SON

*Aloha!
Ana,*

Cecilia Johansen

CECILIA JOHANSEN

Cover image "A Fishing Canoe off North Kona"
Copyright © 1984 Herbert K. Kāne, LLC

PAGE PUBLISHING, INC.
New York, NY

First originally published by Page Publishing, Inc. 2016

ISBN 978-1-68289-491-0 (pbk)
ISBN 978-1-68289-492-7 (digital)

Printed in the United States of America

To

Bernard Albert (Al) ʻEleu wawā kinikini ka
noho ʻana kau hale mehameha* Johansen
and Charles (Kāne) Kanewa
Waipa cousins of Kapaʻahu, Puna, Hawaiʻi
whose stories and songs kept me constantly entertained
and
desirous of knowing and understanding
more of the beautiful
Hawaiian culture they shared with me.
I am forever grateful to them.

Aloha wau iā ʻoe, Al and Kāne. Mahalo nui loa.

Bernard Albert Johansen
(July 30, 1932, to October 29, 2009)
Charles Hikuokalani Kanewa
(April 1, 1933, to November 2, 2003)

*The lonely but ambitious warrior who went from village to village. Every one he goes to, the villagers bring gifts to his feet. (An inoa kāhea—calling name—given him by his mother.)

Mahalo nui loa

to

Leona Leialoha
Maile Waipā Carr
Marge White
Hōkūlani Holt
Mākela M. Bruno-Kidani
Bud Boland
Susan Switzer
Waimea Writers' Support Group

CONTENTS

PREFACE

Bernard Albert "Al" Johansen was born in 1932 in Kapaʻahu, district of Puna, on Hawaiʻi Island. His father Bernard Johansen Sr. was born in Norway. His mother Elizabeth Waiaʻu Waipa was born in Kapaʻahu of Limaloa Waipa and Lucy Kahikina Kaukini was from Wood Valley above Pahala on the slopes of Mauna Loa.

His father, coming from the Victorian era, subjected Al to the harsh discipline of the times as he himself had been disciplined. It was not altogether fair and a complete contrast to his mother, who was strict in the Hawaiian fashion of the work ethic but was nevertheless loving and kind.

Al was the eldest of six children and the first live birth of his parents. They were married in 1925 and adopted two sons before Al was born. He did not know his brothers well as they were older and left home early and were subjected to the same discipline Bernard Sr. had been.

Al's story is a little history of one small part of the geography of the Hawaiian Islands. Hawaiʻi Island was rich in the musical world for turning out such artists as Ledward and Nedward Kaʻapana and their cousin Dennis Pavao of Hui ʻOhana fame and Uncle Fred Punahoa, a leading slack-key artist who influenced many brilliant guitarists of today. In reality, there were many artists who were never recorded but nevertheless created a kind of music as nowhere else in the world. Because there was no electricity in the area of Kapaʻahu and Kalapana, what entertainment they did have was unique and enjoyable and made the long hours of work bearable.

The last thirty years has seen the destruction of Kapaʻahu and most of Kalapana by Madame Pele. In her volcanic exuberance, she has reclaimed that ʻāina as her own.

My husband had a project he'd dreamed about for years when I met him in 2004. However, his eyesight was taken from him by macular degeneration making it impossible for him to do the required research for the novel he wished to write. I tried to help him bring to life his idea of "a Hawaiian boy in the late 1700s sailing onboard one of the many ships sent out from European or American ports for exploration and trade. He would live with the Indians of the Pacific Northwest Coast and make canoes."

Those ships sailed around Cape Horn from the Atlantic and into the Pacific, making the convenient stopover at the Sandwich Islands for food and water. The circle route then took them to the Northwest Coast to China and back again.

The boy of the story—a canoe maker's son and being curious of sea and land—took great interest in those large ships. They were bigger than the biggest double-hulled canoes talked about since that first landing of Captain Cook at Kealakekua Bay on the leeward side of Hawaiʻi Island. So this is the story. Let us begin.

PROLOGUE

Waimānalo, O'ahu—the Present Day

The announcement came to fasten seat belts for the landing at Honolulu Airport, and George Keola obeyed without thought. The only things on his mind were his family at home in Waimānalo and his grandfather, the man they all called Papa in the hospital with a heart attack. Downing the last swallow of his Jack Daniels, he dropped his cup in the trash bag the stewardess held before him.

"Thank you, Sergeant," she said, smiling. "We're very proud of you, and our airline is happy to transport you home."

* * * * *

The old man sat on the pier with a fishing pole in one hand, absentmindedly fingering the nylon line with the other. The morning sun felt hot on his back and glinted off lapping waves caressing his ankles. His grandson was coming home from military service that day.

George Keola, who Papa called Keoki, had been in the Marine Corps for twenty years and was retiring at thirty-eight years old. The old man smiled, thinking what a fine man his grandson had become. He himself had been in the U.S. Army fighting in Korea then reenlisting in the Marine Corps, seeing action in Vietnam, and retiring after thirty years. He loved the military and was pleased that his son Kamuela and grandson Keoki had followed in his footsteps. Both had been in combat in the Middle East.

Suddenly, the line pulled hard and the old man jerked the pole. The battle began.

"Pull him up, Papa! Pull him up," a voice shouted from behind.

The old man recognized his grandson's voice but didn't stop to acknowledge it. His brow was dripping with perspiration as he pulled with all his strength to get the fighting fish out of the water. Suddenly, an ulua was flopping in his hand. Papa removed the hook from its mouth and placed it in the bucket.

"He mea'ai kēia no kēia ahiahi!" he said while his grandson helped him up.

Keoki smiled as he heard the old Hawaiian language. Yes, it would be good eating that night.

The two men shook hands, embraced, and at arm's length, assessed each other. The grandson, tall and broad, looked quite handsome in his utility uniform.

"You look so much like my dad when he was your age," Papa said.

Keoki smiled broadly with the compliment, his face creased where dimples should have been.

The grandfather, however, looked much older since the last time Keoki saw him. But he was still tall and lanky and as Marine Corps straight as his eighty-three years would allow, no beer-belly 'ōpū for him. The old uniform was kept cleaned and pressed and no doubt would still fit when he was laid in his coffin. Granddad's hair was hanging on his forehead as it had always done. Even though he combed it just so like when he was in the Marines, it was poker straight and never stayed in place even with his cover, an old baseball cap.

The old man shuffled a bit until he got his legs under him while Keoki picked up the bucket and other gear lying on the dock. "I thought you were in the hospital. It's a good thing I called Tūtū. She said you were fishing. I couldn't believe it. What are you doing here?"

The old man winced at the lecture. "It was just angina," he said as if it were nothing. "They kept me overnight and gave me more pills. I'm okay."

"Tūtū Kanani, we're on our way," Keoki spoke to his grandmother on the cell phone as they got into the car. "Yes, Papa got a nice bucket full of fish and some 'a'ama."

By the time they reached the grandparents' Waimānalo home for the welcome home lū'au, Granddad had fallen asleep. A little unnerved, Keoki gently shook the slumped shoulder. "Papa, Papa, we're here."

The house was crowded with guests. Family and friends spilled out into the garage and tents had been set up for the occasion. Smoke from the barbecue rose in great circles over the house, and the smell made Keoki's mouth water. He smiled with pleasure as he saw his wife coming out of the house with more food. She smiled back but was lost in the crowd of guests.

Keoki greeted old friends and some of his Marine Corps buddies. There were family members he hadn't seen for years and some he'd never seen before—so many babies and young children. They seemed to be everywhere, and his five-year-old twins Kanalu and Ku'ulei were right in the middle of them all.

Then Papa found Tūtū Kanani sitting by the back door on the lānai. She gave him a little squeeze, and Keoki smiled, amazed that they were still in love after sixty-three years of marriage. He tried to get back to greet his grandmother, but suddenly, Kanalu and Kuʻulei discovered their daddy was home and demanded to be picked up. His arms were full of wiggling babies, and his cheeks were covered with wet kisses. His wife Liana made it through the noisy celebration to plant a loving kiss on her husband's lips. He longed to hold her in his arms, but she gave him a knowing look and whispered, "Later!" He could hardly wait. She was so beautiful. Her tank top barely concealed her curves, and her long black hair curled around her shoulders teasingly.

The boys from the neighborhood arrived with their instruments, and the party took off. Papa's contribution of fresh fish and that large black crab he caught—much loved by the locals—were cooked alongside steaks and ribs on the barbecue. Of course, there was the usual lūʻau fare: kālua pork and cabbage; laulau of succulent pork and butterfish in their packet of ti leaves; chicken long rice; chicken and squid lūʻau, thick and sweet with coconut milk; lomi salmon, tomatoes and onions; melt-in-your-mouth poke; and salads and desserts. Papa was already eating poi with his fingers.

"Where's the ʻopihi?" Keoki asked him as he put the children down.

"No more! All pau," he said sadly with a wave of his hand.

So it was true—the limpets were extinct. Keoki couldn't believe it. The taro was nearly wiped out with years of genetic modifying, but some farmers in the deep inaccessible valleys of the islands had quietly managed to save the original strain and made poi for a select list of Hawaiians.

"Ah," Keoki thought, "I can't wrap my mind around that today!"

The blare of the music had died down so Keoki could hardly hear it. Someone was singing "Moanalua," and Aunty Becky was dancing the beautiful hula, ruffles of her red holomū gently brushing the floor as she dipped and swayed. Kamuela handed him his guitar. Keoki played pretty good kīhoʻalu, but his dad had been the expert in the old style of Fred Punahoa from Kalapana back in the day. Keoki sat in for a few numbers until his third beer ran out. He was getting pretty hungry and found Liana among the guests for some good grinds joined by the rest of the Keola family: his step-mom Dee Dee, uncles Bobbie and Micah, and Keoki's twin cousins Franklin and Marshall. All the ʻohana was here. It was very good to be home.

The party began to wane, and Papa went off to take a nap. The women started putting away the leftover food in the kitchen and some of the guys went out for more beer. Keoki found himself very tired. He'd been up since five o'clock California time in order to catch the plane to Honolulu, and it was very warm in the house. He didn't have any trouble falling asleep.

Liana let her husband rest even though the party began again in earnest, and the music started up above eardrum comfort. Some of the gang showed up from Kailua, and a few Marine Corps buddies came from Kāneʻohe. They stayed awhile then told Liana they'd see her husband the next day. Neighbors from down Huli Street came with more food—stew and Portuguese bean soup—and one of the kids went out for fried chicken. Keoki was out like a light.

The house was very still when Keoki woke up. He guessed everyone was gone but thought he could hear voices in the living room when he went to the kitchen for water. Liana came in when she heard her husband at the sink.

"Oh, you're up! Did you have a good sleep?"

"Yeah, I sure was tired," he said, yawning.

"You hungry? There's some soup on the stove."

"Sure, baby." She started to the cabinet for a bowl, but he caught her in his arms and kissed her. "Finally, a moment alone." Going for a can of beer in the cooler, he said, "Later."

Liana pretended shyness, but there was a seductive sparkle in her eyes. "Go inside. I'll bring it to you."

Aunty Becky was still with Papa, bending his ear, and Tūtū was caressing Ku'ulei's hair as she sat curled in the crook of her great-grandmother's arm, eyes heavy with sleep. Kanalu's chin was nearly on his chest, and he was snoring just loud enough to block out the ten-o'clock news.

"I guess I'd better put them to bed," Liana said.

"Wait, I'll help," Papa said, looking for any excuse to get away from his sister's chatter.

She picked up Ku'ulei, and Papa carried Kanalu right behind her down the hall to the guest bedroom. Of course, the minute they were put in bed with their blankets tucked up around their necks, both children awoke and demanded a story. Liana said it was too late and that they should go to sleep, but they demanded all the louder.

"Tell us a story. Tell us a story."

Papa could see the dark circles under Liana's eyes and said, "I'll do it." Then he whispered, "I'll probably bore them to sleep!" She smiled and left the room.

"Well now, what would you like to hear?" He reached for one of their books on the nightstand.

"Tell us a new one," Kanalu said. "Yeah, a new one," repeated his sister.

"Oh…well…let me think. It's been a long time since your father and grandfather were little, and I told them stories." They looked at each other in amazement that their father and grandfather were little once. The old man smiled and began, "Once upon a time, there was a boy who loved horses." The children loved horses and were wide-eyed.

"Who, Papa, who?"

"They looked like little owls, the pueo that flew over the pastures on Hawai'i Island," the old man thought smiling. "Oh, a young boy a long…long…time…ago…" He stretched out the words tauntingly.

"Who?" they squealed in delight.

"Me!"

"Oh, oh," he thought, "now I've done it—they're really wide awake!"

"When I was about your size," he began in earnest, "my daddy had a beautiful horse named Prince. He was all white with a long tail and mane, and every morning before work, daddy would lead him out to the pasture ma kai (toward the sea) of Tūtū Limaloa's house to graze. In the evening when daddy came home from work in Hilo town, the first thing he'd do was whistle and slap the side of the feed bucket for Prince to come home to eat his oats. The oats would get stuck all over Prince's soft muzzle, and he'd fuss with his tongue to try to get the tasty bits then he'd take long drinks from the trough."

The children laughed.

Papa continued, "One day, daddy gave me Prince to take care of, and oh, how I loved that beautiful horse. Of course, I was too small to ride him, but we became very attached to each other, and as I grew, I could brush Prince and ride him down the road and show him off to all my friends.

"My cousin Charlie was green with envy and wanted very much to ride him, so one day, I rode up to Charlie's house, and he climbed the fence and hopped on behind me. We had such great fun riding Prince. One day, Charlie's Tūtū man gave him a pinto with one blue eye and one pink eye. He called her Ole Blue Eye, and we rode together a lot, laughing all the way down the road to the Kalapana store. You knew when a car was coming on that one lane road because the horses would hear it three or four miles away. Twenty minutes later, you moved over to the side of the road so the car could pass.

"Charlie's Tūtū also had a great red horse called Huapala, but he traded him for a cow and a calf. We felt bad about it, but he said it would be better because you could get more benefit raising cows than that big horse."

"What's Huapala, Papa?" Kanalu asked, yawning loudly.

"That's Hawaiian for ripe fruit," the old man told them not paying the least bit of attention to the yawn. He continued his reminiscences.

"One time, my daddy and I went to get wild horses at Sheriff Kawaha's place at South Point in Ka'ū, and we stayed overnight. The moonlight on the land and the ocean was so beautiful. I had never seen anything like it. The next day, the men of the ranch rounded up the horses and put them in the back of the big truck. We kept the horses on our ma uka, the mountainside, of our one-acre lot until breaking time.

"I got a lesson in how to break horses from daddy and Tūtū Man Makaliʻi. They were on horses and each had a rope around the neck of a wild horse and led it to a tree where it was saddled. Then the horse was led to our goldfish pond on the ma kai property where it was pulled into the water. Daddy transferred to the back of the wild horse and threw the rope of his horse to me, and I pulled it out of the water. He rode the bucking horse in the water until it stopped. And that's how daddy broke in his horses before he sold them."

The old man realized the children were fast asleep.

"Well, I finally did it," he said as he sighed. Pulling up their covers, he discovered that he'd sat too long and his legs were stiff. His wife was at the doorway.

"Damn, I'm getting too old for this…How long you been standing there?" he whispered.

"Turn off the light, old man, and come to bed." She was in her nightgown and still looked pretty even at eighty years old.

"How long we been married?" he asked.

"Oh, who cares. Long enough I guess. Let's go to bed. What were you telling those children? Some of those old war stories?" Kanani noticed her husband's hair on his forehead again!

"Naw, just some horse tales. They were bored enough— they fell asleep."

She laughed and brushed that wayward lock out of his face. He reached for the hall light switch, turned it off, and took his wife in his arms. She feigned shyness, but his arms tightened all the more around her. He kissed her lips, and she responded to his passion.

She brushed his ear with a whisper, "Let's go to bed."

The next morning, the children were wild with excitement. They didn't even have to be called to the kitchen for their breakfast. Liana was amazed and wondered aloud to her husband, "What the heck did Papa tell the kids last night? I've never seen them like this." Kanalu was running around his mother in circles as she tried to set the table.

"Hey, boy, what's the matter with you?" Keoki stopped him in his tracks.

The two were standing together, afraid they would be punished. Ku'ulei had tried to put her hair in ponytails but didn't manage to get them quite even, one was down, the other up. The little wisps of 'ehu—reddish-brown—hair curled around her face, and the boy's hair flattened out in the back, gitty-gitty style. That cowlick was never to be tamed. Liana smiled at their new looks.

"Did you wash your hands and face this morning?" They ignored her altogether.

"Papa told the most exciting stories about a big white horse and how he fed it and rode it and old blue eye and old pink eye and, and…"

"Whoa, slow down, Kanalu."

"But, daddy, there was the moon and a red horse, huli pali, or something like that."

"Huapala, Kanalu," Papa corrected him as he came in from the back yard. "I'm hungry. Where's mama?"

Papa looked especially nice that morning. He was clean-shaven and didn't smell of fish from yesterday. Tūtū always tried to help him pick out his clean clothes for the day because the seat of his pants was always dirty from sitting on the heels of his rubber boots when he worked in the yard.

"I was washing clothes, old man. Where do you think I was?" she said coming in from the garage, sneering at him with an armload of clothes.

Cereal was in the bowls and waiting for the kids, and Liana put the pot of rice on the table for the adults. That morning, a big platter of eggs and Portuguese sausage awaited them and sliced papaya from the tree in the yard.

"What were you telling them last night, Dad?" Liana asked her grandfather-in-law.

"Oh, just some tales about when I grew up—"

Just then, the phone interrupted Papa's sentence. It was an invitation for Keoki to go to Kāne'ohe Marine Corps Base for lunch with those buddies he'd missed at the party. After his retirement at Camp Pendleton in California, he was placed on the Fleet Reserve list for ten years. If necessary, he could be called up again.

"Well, I'd better go." He kissed Liana's cheek. "Papa, I'd like to hear some of your stories soon."

"Sure, sure," the old man said.

Everyone went their separate ways, and the women began to clean up. Tūtū's dishwasher made things go fast.

Keoki's day was longer than he thought it would be. By the time he reached his grandparents' place, it was nearly dinnertime. His mind ran back to the kids' talk about their great-grandfather's stories.

"Papa's not here," Liana told her husband. "He had a poker game over at Sol's place."

Some nights later, Papa was called on again to help put the little ones to sleep. They clamored for another story, and the old man scratched his head.

"Well, my mama used to gather honey. Would you like to hear about that?"

"Gather honey?" they asked in unison. The honey they knew came in cute plastic bottles that looked like a teddy bear, and their mom put it on toast.

"When I was your age in Kapa'ahu, mama and I—"

Kanalu interrupted the story, "Kapa...what's Kapa, Papa?" Kuʻulei mimicked her brother "Kapa_Papa, Kapa Papa," they kept saying it over and over again.

He was getting irritated and raised his voice, "Do you want to hear the story or not?" Their little eyes got big when they heard his deep bass voice. Just then, Tūtū walked by their bedroom door.

"Papa, don't frighten those children with your Marine Corps voice!"

"Sorry, now, do you want to hear the story?" Both children nodded.

"When I was seven or eight and still living in Kapaʻahu, my mama and I would go in the morning down to the crack in the lava on our land looking for beehives. She lit a torch, which would smoke wildly from the kerosene-soaked rice bag and waved it in the small caves to chase away the bees. Mama handed me the torch and reached in to grab the honeycomb. She cut the comb in pieces, dropping them in the bucket. At home, we squeezed out the honey. Mama would still have bees in her hair. We dipped breadfruit, taro, and sometimes, sweet potato into the honey. It was real ʻono! Second to none!"

By that time, Keoki and Liana were standing outside the bedroom door listening. They looked at each other, and Liana whispered into her husband's ear, "We've got to get this down. I've never heard Papa's stories before." Keoki nodded. Then the phone rang and Liana ran to get it. Keoki went after her to get a drink while Papa continued the story with the children.

The next day, Papa had an important follow-up medical appointment scheduled after the angina scare. However, the family never got a chance to sit down and talk about the stories, and Liana wanted to start looking for a place of their own.

The couple found a house in the town of Enchanted Lake right across the street from an elementary school. That lake in ancient times was a fish pond called Kaʻelepulu. Papa's stories were put on the back burner as everyone settled into their new roles.

One day, shortly after Keoki and Liana moved into their new home, they received a call from Aunty Becky saying that Papa's good poker buddy Sol, had suddenly died. He was pronounced dead of an aneurysm at Queen's Hospital in Honolulu. Keoki was in shock. He knew Sol had been Papa's friend from their childhood in Kapaʻahu on Hawaiʻi Island. Unknown to him, however, was the fact that Aunty Becky and Papa were actually second cousins to Sol. The funeral was to be held the following week.

A get together at Sol's home followed the service. Keoki met the family who all lived on the mainland. They were drinking beer and smoking in the back yard, but Keoki kept hearing over and over how they regretted not getting the story of their father's life. One after another, they asked the very questions Keoki had been asking a few months before. He only knew where Papa was born, but that was the limit of his knowledge of his grandfather's heritage. He swore under his breath then repeated his thoughts later to his wife. They stopped at a fast-food restaurant after leaving the gathering because the kids were clamoring for chicken nuggets.

"Liana," Keoki started saying over his coffee, "we have to sit down with Papa and Tūtū before it's too late. Sol's funeral was a wake-up call for me."

"Me too," Liana spoke softly. "Set it up, and I'll record him."

Papa got real quiet over the weeks following Sol's death, and Keoki didn't think he would ever open up again.

But Granddad surprised him one night after Tūtū had a heart-to-heart with her husband. All Papa said was "Come over."

When Granddad's sister Becky heard about the stories, her daughter Leona suggested they have a family reunion. Keoki and Liana really liked the idea, and even though Granddad protested at first, he began to realize he hadn't seen his other two sisters in a long time. Also, there were many grandchildren and great-grandchildren he'd never seen. Suddenly, the whole family was excited with the prospect.

In the coming months, e-mail and text messages were sent back and forth as the events of the reunion to be held on Hawai'i Island were arranged. There was to be a big banquet on Saturday night and trips planned to the graves of the kūpuna (ancestors), a caravan tour down to the lava-covered homeland and visits to related families and friends in the new Kalapana subdivision. Last minute details were ironed out, and the trip was a go!

Tears fell from Granddad's eyes when he stepped off the plane in Hilo. After sixty-three years, the fragrance of his home island of Hawai'i flooded his mind with memories of his mother's long black hair, perfumed with her favorite 'awapuhi ke'oke'o, the white ginger she wore behind her ear or at Sunday church—a woven flower lei po'o for her head, the coconut trees he'd climbed to get the *spoon meat* of the young nuts with their delicious refreshing water, and the heady scent of plumeria that grew around his parents' home. Even the smell of the sea was somehow different.

Keoki noticed his grandfather wiping his face with his handkerchief. "You okay, Papa?"

"Yeah, just sweating that's all…" his voice trailed off. Keoki hoped the trip wasn't too strenuous for him.

Family came from all over, and when they arrived at the hotel, each person was given an itinerary of events. The first night was a service at the old Mary Star of the Sea Church in Kalapana. It had been saved from the lava flow in 1993 when it was physically moved off its foundation and out of harm's way.

At the Saturday night lū'au, Leona asked Granddad to say grace before everyone ate. Keoki walked with him and helped him to the stage then adjusted the microphone for him. Falteringly, Granddad began. Keoki was afraid he would get cold feet, but the old man coughed and continued. He said he would say grace but wanted everyone to say the Lord's Prayer together first.

E kō mākou Makua i loko o ka lani
E hoʻāno ʻia Kou inoa
E hiki mai Kou aupuni
E mālama ʻia Kou makemake ma ka honua nei
E like me ia i mālama ʻia ma ka lani lā
E hāʻawi mai iā mākou i kēia lā, i ʻai na mākou
    no nēia lā
E kala mai hoʻi iā mākou i ka mākou lawehala ʻana
Me mākou e kala nei i ka poʻe i lawehala i kā mākou
Mai hoʻokuʻu ʻoe iā mākou i ka hoʻowalewale ʻia mai
E hoʻopakele nō naʻe iā mākou i ka ʻino
No ka mea, Nou ke aupuni, a me ka mana
A me ka hoʻonani ʻia ā mau loa aku
ʻĀmene. (Kamehameha Schools)

None of the young ones knew it in Hawaiian except those keiki in the immersion schools, but Tūtū grasped hands with Kamuela on her left and a cousin to her right, and the prayer gradually went around the room. The words were coming back to those who knew them and those who didn't listened quietly to grasp the old Hawaiian language. When the prayer was ending, all arms reached to the heavens for the last two lines. Papa then thanked God for what they were about to enjoy and asked a blessing on all the Keola family.

Through the course of the meal, local musicians performed, and later, a kani ka pila started with others joining the group. After dessert was served, most of the young people went outside, and the older ones renewed acquaintances with cousins they had not seen for years.

Leona invited Granddad's sisters to get up and speak to the crowd about their experiences back in the day.

Then it was Papa's turn. Leona had been waiting for that moment for a very long time. He began with the small bedtime stories Keoki recognized, but other stories began flooding from his Granddad like a dam that held back decades of water. A small crack suddenly opened to a full-on deluge.

Liana let the camcorder continue to run hoping the battery would hold out, but Granddad saved her the worry—his battery ran low as his voice gave out.

The next day, Granddad's vigor returned, and everyone was enjoying the new Kaimū Beach State Park. Some years before the lava stopped flowing there, and a residential development began anew in the Kalapana Estates area right on top of the old lava field. A beautiful new pavilion was built, and visitors were able to enjoy the black sand beach again. Ferns grew and many coconut palms were planted by visitors. The area became postcard perfect once more.

As they were enjoying their lunch, Leona asked Granddad to tell more stories. He was feeling very relaxed from drinking 'awa that one of his old buddies brought.

"I want to tell you a story, Georgie, that I have never told before." There was an urgency in his voice.

"My great-great-great-grandfather 'Eleu was born in 1773." He paused, watching his grandson's face light up with excitement. "He grew up to be a canoe maker just like his father before him. They both were in service to Kalaniʻōpuʻu, the great chief of Hawaiʻi Island."

Tūtū Kanani was trying to corral some of the littlest great-grandchildren and heard what her husband said. She smiled, knowing at last that he could tell someone else the story.

"Not only were they canoe makers to the king, but ʻEleu went to the Pacific Northwest Coast on a great tall ship."

"What? Papa, I can't believe it."

"It is true, boy. Now, let me tell the story of the canoe maker's son."

KAPA'AHU, HAWAI'I ISLAND— THE ANCIENT PAST

THE CANOE MAKER'S SON (1778)

The boy felt some rebellion when his mother told him to go to bed. Sunset had been spectacular with shafts of sun shooting through brilliant gold-rimmed cumulus clouds. He watched the play of light and shadow rolling across land and sea. But darkness was descending fast over the ahupua'a, the land division where they lived, and he lit his little kukui[1] nut torch with a glowing ember from the fire. Not wanting to end the day just yet, he thought back on the men's talk about the day's happenings: canoe surfing, fishing, 'opihi picking, a new hale (house) for a newly wedded couple, methods of repairing a crumbling heiau (temple) wall, and finding the best koa trees to make the best canoes. Those things kept playing in his young mind. Would he ever be old enough to do the things the men did?

---

1.   Candlenut

He sat down in front of his 'ohana's sleeping hale and gazed toward the heavens where a million stars seemed to appear out of nowhere. He wondered about those millions of stars and a million other things. Slowly, however, fingers of gauzy clouds began swallowing the smallest stars and then the brightest. The moon rose in the east, and he heard an 'ohe hanu ihu (nose flute) and a nī'au kani (singing splinter) off in the distance possibly from two lovers in different villages, but the boy was not sure for his eyes grew heavy with sleep. His last kukui nut burnt out.

He awoke in his mother's hale to his father's soft chanting. He scrambled to his feet, splashed water on his face from a gourd hanging on the peg outside the hale, and washed the maka piapia from his eyes. He hurried to his father's side. He was late, but his father never missed a note of the chant, the ancient oli, to correct his son. The rise and fall of his rich bass voice with its strong vibrato filled the hale mua and caused the boy to thrill with excitement, and he wondered if he could ever follow in his father's footsteps with his small voice. He vowed he would never again be late to learn the important chants of his 'ohana.

His father was a warrior and a fine canoe maker. His canoes were sought after by many chiefs, but his heart was at the side of ali'i nui Kalani'ōpu'u. The great chief called him *Kanewa* for his fearlessness in battle with the war club and his use of the adze in making his excellent canoes. The boy was too young for such things although he and his friends played at mock battles with sticks.

"Where were you, 'Eleu?" his father asked after finishing his oli.

"I was dreaming of the tall ships that came to Kaua'i after the Makahiki festival. Canoes were sent to spread the news to all the islands. The messengers said that our god Lono had returned on great moku. The sails were so big and the moku so high, and I wanted to see those trees floating on the water and—"

His father stopped him. "'Eleu, you must be prompt to learn all the necessary things we do in our lives."

"Yes, my makua kāne." The boy hung his head for he hated disappointing his father.

"Come, boy, we must start the imu (underground oven) for your mother's food. This is the way of our life, and you are old enough now to begin learning these things."

Kanewa turned away and began preparing fish wrapped in lū'au leaves, and kalo to steam for his family's poi. In a second imu, he would prepare his own breakfast. 'Eleu would eat with his mother for a while longer then he would join his father and the men of the ahupua'a in a special ceremony. The kapu directing the kānaka lives was strong. The boy had to understand all these rules and regulations. He would learn by watching.

After their morning meal, Kanewa had to gather some items to prepare for the day ahead. 'Eleu was on his heels like an 'īlio, a puppy underfoot, in his father's face and not being any help at all.

"What are you doing, 'Eleu?"

"I'm learning by watching, makua kāne."

"Hiki nō, all right." In desperation, Kanewa said to his son, "Hele 'oe pā'ani, 'Eleu."

The boy ran off to play with five-year-old Keola, 'Eleu's best friend.

Their most fun in the world was to he'e hōlua or go down the slide on papa hōlua, the sled. The hōlua had been on their ahupua'a from ancient times. It was a very long slide, and the boys would get a running start and flop down on top of the sled as it flew down the ti leaf covered embankment of lava rock. 'Eleu lay silently at the bottom of the slide, ti leaves thrown up over his back and under the sled. He wasn't uncomfortable, though. In fact, he felt exhilarated and full of life. He loved the slide almost as much as being in his father's canoe. The wind in his face and the sun on his bare back when he was rushing down the slope or through the rough surf made his heart pound. Smiling, he opened his eyes to see white billowy clouds float silently across the blue-black sky. Suddenly, Keola went swishing by, rolling over and laughing uncontrollably as ti leaves went flying.

That day, they would launch Kanewa's kingly canoe from Kalapana beach instead of the paepae wa'a, the canoe ladder at Kī. They gathered their tools, kapa for wiping and water gourds and began the two-and-one-half-mile trip with their neighbors Kaimalino and Keola.

Both boys were thrilled at the prospect of launching the canoe with their fathers. The day was absolutely glorious while walking along from Kapa'ahu. The sun glinted off the ocean, and big waves crashed along the pali. Some days, the sea spray was blown by the wind across the trail, but that day, there was just a good land breeze coming off the mountain—the Moani 'Ala—carrying the fragrance of hala. The Puna district was known for the scent of its hala plant.

Their fathers chatted together, but the boys kicked at stones and were only interested in who could kick their stone the farthest. Suddenly, a movement of leaves caught their attention. Many 'ōma'o were in an 'ōhi'a tree, and as they rushed that tree, the birds took off. The Hawaiian thrushs' habit was to fly straight up to the sky singing wildly as they did so.

"How many can you count, Keola?" 'Eleu asked in the new game.

Keola squinted as he looked up. "Seven…no eight. They go so high you can barely see them. Oh, look," he continued, "here they come." All of them dived straight down to another tree far away from the naughty boys.

On the trail, they passed many hale with good-sized kalo and 'uala patches. The kahuna lā'au lapa'au, the local curing expert, Nāihe waved to them as he pulled weeds between his plants. Noticing the two small boys with the men, he motioned for them to come. "E komo mai," he shouted. His wife Anuhea brought out some kō, the sugar cane the boys loved, and they began chewing voraciously—the delicious sweetness flowing down their throats and chins.

Nāihe's dark skin glowed in the summer sun as he talked to the men, his big smile showing the pleasure he felt sharing the news of the day, inquiring if they had seen the king's runner early that morning announcing the great ali'i's visit the next day. Of course, the men knew he would be there to inspect the canoe—a fleet had been commissioned, and

Kanewa's canoe was the last to be tried and tested. Everyone would be there.

Nāihe was well-respected from Kaimū all the way to ʻĀpua. However, the men would not offend him by saying they had already seen the runner. King Kalaniʻōpuʻu's runners, wearing malo, were famous for being able to run flat out so their loincloth would shoot straight out behind them.

When the men and their sons reached the beautiful black sand beach of Kalapana, all the people living nearby were assembled. The crowd included family heads of the ahupuaʻa from Poupou, Kamoamoa, Kahauale'a, Kapa'ahu, Kalapana, and Kaimū[2] and stood on the sandy beach or floated in canoes on the water.

ʻEleu never paid attention to what people looked like, and quite suddenly, he was aware of his father's appearance. Kanewa was his name—the war club. It seemed an odd thing to be called, but his father was a tall strong man with very large hands. "Sort of club-like, I guess," he thought to himself, wrinkling his nose. Hands like that would be desired in his profession. His father was an expert with the adze of all sizes and could flake great large pieces as well as the most delicate of pieces from koa logs of which the canoes were made. He was able to hew out a log faster than any other canoe makers in the district, which made him a favorite of the local chiefs. With that last canoe of the fleet done in record time, he would be the favorite of the great chief Kalaniʻōpuʻu.

ʻEleu noticed how the people respected his father, and when it came time to remove the canoe from its hālau waʻa, the long house built to protect it, the boy immediately felt pride that he was the canoe maker's son—a new feeling for the young boy of five years old.

---

2.   Except for Kalapana, these ahupuaʻa have not survived due to lava flow

The lauhala mats of the big double-hull canoe were removed, and its immense size and luster shocked the people. Each koa hull was seventy-five feet long, and the platform made of ʻōhiʻa would hold at least eighty paddlers.

Kanewa was gone for months in the forest to find a perfect matched pair of koa trees fit for the king, and when they were completed, the outside hulls were painted red below the moʻo (gunwale strakes). Most makers daubed black on their hulls to water-proof them, but red was in honor of the king, and it was a kingly trademark.

The district chief and family heads of the ahupuaʻa joined together to help carry the big canoe. Kanewa took no chances when it came to a waʻa for the king. All must be perfect. The next day was the true test! ʻEleu wondered what the true test was.

Everyone looked on the majestic waʻa admiring kino (body), manu (upper endpieces of bow and stern), moʻo, and wae (u-shaped spreaders)—all paheʻe, smooth as skin. The kahuna chanted the blessing as the beautiful canoe was carried to the water's edge and introduced to the waves of the delightful bay.

Chosen paddlers, headed by Kanewa, jumped with joy into the canoe and together, dipped their paddles into the swell of the blue water. The wood of the canoe, the caulking of ʻulu sap and the lashings of ʻaha, shuddered in the unequal forces of the ocean, causing the men to hold their breath as they timed their strokes precisely. The canoe settled gracefully onto the cresting waves, all the parts working together. They moved slowly at first then with increasing speed, they set their bodies to work. Initially, paddles were entering noiselessly, pulling with no splash then they paddled faster and faster until their bodies glistened with spray as the bows cut through the water. It was a perfect canoe that turned into a wide circle far out into the ocean then returned to the beach. The steersman smiled approvingly. Kanewa watched the swells. The men heard the paddle-tap on the side of the hull, and with a shout, they caught a big wave. The outcry of the excited paddlers and those on the beach was heard far and wide as the seaworthy canoe passed its first test and a great feast was held.

Carried back to its resting place, Kanewa wiped down the canoe with kapa especially prepared for that purpose. The kapa was some of his wife's softest cloth with many layers so it would not fall apart when wet. How proud he was of the gift she had given him. A lustrous shine returned to the canoe's body as Kanewa stroked her. He would sleep with his beauty tonight, and he would prepare to greet his king in the morning.

'Eleu wanted to stay with his father and was disappointed to be returning home with Keola and Kaimalino. Kanewa told 'Eleu that when the king arrived, it was no place for little children.

The sun was low in the sky when 'Eleu came to his mother's hale, crying.

"Don't be sad, my little Lei," she said, pulling him close to her. His arms wound around her neck.

"Why do you call me Lei, my makua wahine?" he asked his mother, wet lashes framing his dark eyes.

"You are my first born, and when you put your arms around my neck, it is like wearing a fragrant lei. I have a surprise for you after we eat our meal."

Their food was leftovers from the morning. They dipped their fingers into delicious poi from the big wooden bowl. Dried 'ōpelu, 'opihi, 'inamona—a mash of kukui nut kernels with salt—and roasted 'uala rounded out the meal. 'Eleu relished every morsel, and afterward, his mother took him outside.

The boy's eyes were as big as 'omo (poi bowl covers) when his mother removed the lauhala mats, and he saw the surprise. It was a small practice canoe with a beautiful koai'a paddle just made for him. His father had hoped it would distract his son when he had to go to Ka'ū with the king.

"This is yours, 'Eleu. I will teach you what you need to know then your father will begin your lessons so you may follow in his footsteps."

'Eleu wasn't quite sure what she meant, but the small canoe excited him.

That night, his mother didn't have to tell 'Eleu to go to bed. He crawled onto her lap, exhausted. The small fire, made to roast fresh 'ōpelu a neighbor had given them, was comforting, and his fringe of eyelashes fluttered closed, finally giving in to sleep. 'Eleu's little chin rested on his chest as the two fish skewered together on the cooking stick hissed and dripped delicious fat into the fire. She ate both fish while watching her sleeping son curled in her lap.

The next morning, she took 'Eleu with his paddle down to Kī where the paepae wa'a rested on the rocky promontory and spilled over the cliff, bobbing in the sea below. Their friend Kaipo helped her launch Kanewa's big fishing canoe. They picked the right swell and pushed off; the mother was paddling as hard as she could to get off the swell before it smashed the canoe backward into the cliff. 'Eleu was amazed at his mother's expertise with the paddle and a little frightened by the ladder launch. He did not need to be told, however, what to do next. With his little paddle, he copied his mother's strokes, watching where she placed her hands and how the paddle was to dip and pull. He was thrilled with the excitement of being in the canoe and the sea spray hitting his face.

Once they were out safely on the water, his mother began to turn northeast toward Kalapana. Would she beach the canoe there or paddle on to Kaimū? 'Eleu didn't know; the task at hand was all he could manage.

His shorter paddle just barely broke the surface, but he pulled with all his might. The paddle didn't quite make it, and he vowed he would grow fast so he could paddle well and pull his own weight.

'Eleu was excited to see the pali for the first time from the ocean. Hakuma[3] ran for two miles toward Kalapana where it gave way to a black sand beach.

His mother steered the canoe to where the swells began then caught a wave, and they landed right on the beach. Some young men fishing with 'upena 'ulu'ulu left those throw nets in the sand and dived in the waves and went body surfing to chase the canoe. It was great fun. Everyone was laughing. Some men pulled the canoe further on shore; one grabbed 'Eleu and swung him high up in the air. Others kissed his mother in the Hawaiian way, honi—touching noses. Those boys were their cousins.

"We will visit my sister," his mother said to 'Eleu.

As they walked along, 'Eleu overheard kūpuna tell his mother that Kanewa had sailed with the great king to Ka'ū last evening and would be back the next day. 'Eleu was disappointed again.

'Eleu's mother was named for the full moon of the night—Kamahinaohōkū. Her sister was Hōkūpa'a, named after the dependable North Star that guided the ancestors from Hawaiki to Hawai'i. When that story was recounted in the evening around kukui nut torches, the small fire in the darkness reflected interest, delight, humor or sadness on every face depending on whether the story contained star-crossed lovers, lost canoes or lost lives.

---

3.   Hakuma horst: a block of the earth's crust separated by faults from adjacent relatively depressed blocks

The two sisters were given their names by their grandfather Ka'ōka'i, kahuna of their birth ahupua'a of Kawaihae. The oldest was called Hōkūpa'a because of how quick she was to hear and remember things taught to her: the long mo'okū'auhau (the family's genealogy chant), hula, lei making, and weaving. She was rock-steady as she went about her tasks and married a man from Kalapana.

Kamahinaohōkū on the other hand had a round face full of light, loved swimming above all else, and was good at paddling. It was fortuitous that she met and fell in love with the handsome canoe maker Kanewa from Kapa'ahu.

On the occasions of visiting her mother and sister, the three sometimes spent time in the Hakūma cave socializing with the other women. It was then that Kamahinaohōkū discovered making kapa was a fun activity. She was dexterous at pounding the fibers of the wauke into the softest of kapa for clothing and bedding. However, she wasn't very artistic and left the decorating to her sister who applied the dyes in eye-catching designs.

While awaiting Kanewa's return, Kamahinaohōkū asked to try her hand at lauhala weaving on a sudden impulse. Her mother had been disgusted that her youngest daughter was forever in the water and had not learned the womanly arts. It was with pride that she saw Kamahinaohōkū twist, bend, and fold her lau to make beautiful and useful things for her home. Even so with the earthy fragrance of the long leaves between her fingers in the cool cave, the aromas of the ocean and 'āina, her land, were all delightful, but the love for the sea was too much. She grew restless with her weaving, sprang up, and flinging off her kihei, dashed for the bright sunlight outside. Kanalu (the waves) were calling, and she could not ignore them. Her mother threw up her arms in frustration.

"Auwē!" she exclaimed. "My daughter," she sighed, while the young and old women shook their heads.

'Eleu went scampering after his mother, throwing off his malo and flinging his little brown nakedness into the cool water to splash with the other keiki. Suddenly, up popped his mother; they were laughing as mother and son enjoyed the fun.

It was growing late, and 'Eleu's stomach was growling. He and his mother joined Hōkūpa'a for their dinner but were interrupted by a ruckus down at the water's edge. One of the boys was shouting that the canoes had returned, and everyone ran down to the beach. 'Eleu saw his father first and ran ahead of his mother. Then Kamahinaohōkū spotted her husband and ran to him to touch noses.

What a grand reunion that night: the men telling stories of the voyage and the royal center at Wai'ahukini in Ka'ū. They brought gifts of food and other useful items. Kalani'ōpu'u, at his favorite fishing center, was pleased with the canoe and took delight in his people and their talent.

Kanewa joined in the retelling of the days' events but could hardly take his eyes off his wife. She was exquisite in the firelight. Her short hair, cut according to Hawaiian custom when her first child 'Eleu was born curled around her face. Her bright dark eyes darted from storyteller to storyteller with excitement, but Kanewa's strong fine-looking features delighted Kamahinaohōkū far more than the stories, and she felt the tug of longing for her husband.

Despite her excitement that the men had returned, she had been harboring a secret for some weeks and was overjoyed to share the news with her husband. She thought it better to wait for the next day as it would be some time before he finished eating and drinking with the men. The normally delectable aroma coming from the men's hale was making her sick, and she knew why! She would remain quietly patient. The fire was still warm as she rested her back against the pili grass hale moe. A sudden gust of makani, however, sent a chill through her. She pulled her kīhei (cape) close around her shoulders and eventually slipped into a gauzy sleep.

Kanewa came out of the hale mua to get water when he found his wife. Kamahinaohōkū awoke with a start at her husband's touch. Tears glistened on her lashes, and he looked at her with alarm.

"I had a bad dream, Kālei," she said, using his 'ohana given name. "It is an omen!" And then trembling, she said, "Ua laulau. I am hāpai." He sat beside his wife, and she felt safe in his embrace. She breathed deeply of the earthy fragrance of her man and her 'āina and thrilled with the new life of Kanewa's next child within her. They touched noses.

He was stunned and excited at the same time. It had been five years since 'Eleu was born keiki 'alu'alu, a premature baby. Kamahinaohōkū's mother had to tell Kanewa he must go to the shore at Kalapana and wash the baby in salt water. There he was, the big strong warrior, standing in the small wavelets, holding the tiny creature gently in one hand and pouring water over the little body with the other.

"E ku'u keiki! My son!" was all Kanewa could muster, fearful he would be too rough. 'Eleu's thin skin would grow normally after many treatments.

The couple had resigned themselves to the fact they might not have more children. They had tried all the usual remedies given them by the kahuna, and even Kamahinaohōkū's sister had offered her youngest child for hānai, but his wife hesitated, and Kanewa wondered why. His nephew was four years old and loved his uncle and aunt. He had been patient for his wife's decision, and finally he understood.

Life went on for the little family of three. Kanewa was busy planting his small garden of kalo, 'uala, and kō, and fishing as his canoe-making skills were not needed at the moment. As the months went on, however, he noticed his wife growing more tired and then very suddenly, her mother died. All the 'ohana came to Kalapana for the burial including Ka'ōka'i, the mother's elderly father from Kawaihae who was a kahuna lā'au lapa'au. Their mother's body had been prepared by the sisters, and the burial had been done in the traditional way. Kamahinaohōkū seemed to give up after that.

'Eleu spent his days crying for his mother, and the time for him to be sent to the men's hale was put on hold as Kanewa didn't want to separate mother and son just yet. Ka'ōka'i came back to Kapa'ahu with them and stayed for a while to help his ailing granddaughter.

Kamahinaohōkū was getting close to her time, but she was strained by her mother's death. Even the short trip to Kalapana tired her out. She begged for her sister, and Kanewa sent a canoe for her. Their mother would have normally helped at the birthing process, but with Hōkūpa'a and Ka'ōka'i, Kanewa was certain that his wife would pull through.

It wasn't to be however. Even with prayer and offerings to the 'aumākua, Kamahinaohōkū died with the still-born baby in her arms. Kanewa mourned them with tears and anguish, a loss so terrible it ripped out his heart. Then he became angry with the gods. What had he left out or forgotten to do to appease them? He clenched his fists, cast those gods away, and swore to worship the only god he could see— King Kalani'ōpu'u. Little 'Eleu did not understand the grief he felt nor could he understand why he could find no comfort with his father.

Ka'ōka'i did what he could, but he finally confronted Kanewa with a proposition. Instead of sending the boy back to Kalapana to live with Hōkūpa'a's family, Ka'ōka'i suggested he take the boy to Kawaihae and bring up 'Eleu in his own hale mua. Ka'ōka'i had trained many young boys of their family to be men. Because he was dead in his heart, Kanewa had no objection.

As the 'ohana's canoes paddled from Kalapana out to sea, 'Eleu watched Kanewa turn and walk away from the sandy beach. He could not see the tears in Kanewa's eyes nor would he see his father again for a very long time. Ka'ōka'i sighed with sadness and turned the boy to face forward.

Kawaihae was hot and dry, not at all like verdant Kapa'ahu. The Mumuku wind from the mountain conflicted with the Nāulu wind from the sea, and it was hard to stay cool under the coconut trees. 'Eleu became a good swimmer!

In the course of growing and learning, 'Eleu's memories were pushed to the back of his mind, but he often wondered what had happened to his happy life with his mother and father. Once in a while he thought of the beautiful little canoe his father had made him. It was all gone, but Ka'ōka'i always pointed his great-grandson forward saying, "Don't dwell on the past, 'Eleu!"

'Eleu had been with Ka'ōka'i for a few months and had just turned six years old when a monumental event took place. It was February 1779 and again the end of the ancient festival of Makahiki when two ships sailed into Kawaihae Bay. Word of the sightings flew round the villages and canoes were launched. Captain Cook had returned on his third voyage. Boats were lowered from the ships. "Load the canoes with fat pigs and vegetables," the people shouted. Hao was to be traded for the island produce, "so take your best." The kānaka knew about iron and coveted it even before Captain Cook arrived.

'Eleu and a twelve-year-old friend Wai'aha were fishing in the bay in a small canoe with Ka'ōka'i. They saw the ships and the boats being lowered. Ka'ōka'i told the boys the men were probably coming ashore to get water because he could see casks being lowered from the decks. Ka'ōka'i and Wai'aha began paddling with all their might to join with other canoes launched from the shore.

Before it came, the great-grandfather could smell it. A huge storm was brewing above their heads. Many of the canoes including theirs were out in the bay surrounding the ships. The wind got stronger, and the ocean became choppy with high waves beginning to form. Suddenly, some canoes capsized, and people floundering in the water were crying for help. Those closest to the shore either paddled or swam and made it back safely. The ships' boats were just making the landing before the storm broke, but then they were faced with an enormous crisis of swamping canoes and drowning people. The lead man of the shore party had his men turn their boats around to try to stop the disaster. His men and the sailors from the ships began to pluck the Sandwich Islanders from the water.

Meanwhile, Kaʻōkaʻi had tied ʻEleu under a nohona waʻa to keep him from being swept overboard, but the canoe began to sink from the heavy seas. Suddenly, one of the ship's boats was alongside fetching Waiʻaha and Kaʻōkaʻi from the swamped canoe and untying little ʻEleu from under the seat. The canoe sunk, the paddles floated away, and ʻEleu's eyes were wide with fear. He watched the canoe disappearing under the waves then looked into the eyes of the big white man in whose arms he rested. The recovered Sandwich Islanders were taken on board *HMS Discovery* and ʻEleu was placed in the arms of a woman. He was dazed, but when he realized he was on that great moku—the ship he'd been dreaming about—he forgot all fear. Eventually, the storm subsided, but not before many of the bedraggled rescued ones had become seasick in the big rocking ship. It was a grand adventure and one ʻEleu would remember all of his life, especially the man who rescued the three of them. His name was Bligh.

'Eleu was with the kāne and learning to become a man. He was taught his moʻokūʻauhau. He was taught to plant the good kalo and ʻuala that would sustain his people. He was taught to paddle and to fish. It was good fishing at Kawaihae, and 'Eleu loved it.

It was late summer of 1782. The shadows of coconut palm fronds touched the ʻāina and shaded the faces of Kaʻōkaʻi and 'Eleu. If not for a slight makani wafting over them, the hot afternoon would have taken their breath away. But the boy paid no attention to the heat. He was intently watching the old man mending one of his many ʻupena and trying to learn the intricacies of hiʻa ka ʻupena, (shuttle made of kauila wood), weaving the olonā fiber back and forth through the tight mesh.

That net would catch small fish. But the old man's gnarled fingers were making mistakes on just about every turn and tie of that shuttle. Annoyed, he gave up and put the net aside.

"Are you troubled, my kupuna kuakahi?" 'Eleu fretted, noting the painful expression on his great-grandfather's face.

Kaʻōkaʻi smiled at his sympathetic great-grandson and touched his shoulder. He was a good boy and not vexed easily, and he always showed concern and love for the old man. "I was hoping I could show you some mending today but no. Let us go home for our dinner. We must gather what we need for a long trip to the mountain tomorrow, and you must begin your training in canoe making. 'Eleu, it is time to build a canoe."

'Eleu was excited about the trip, but the idea lingered in him that there was something more worrisome in his great-grandfather's tone. The thought was cut short when Kaʻōkaʻi pointed to the net and 'Eleu knew he must gather it and put away the implements used in its repair.

The next morning after their meal, they packed dried fish and paʻi ai, the delicious dried poi so prized for the trail, and ʻahu lāʻī, the dried ti leaf cape for the cold. They took Kaʻōkaʻi's sharp koʻi, adzes great and small for cutting and shaping the koa and ʻōhiʻa logs. ʻEleu's wrinkled brow carried an unspoken question about those dried ti leaves, but it went unanswered as they met with Waiʻaha and other ʻohana who would be traveling with them.

Kaʻōkaʻi was silent as they began the twelve-mile hike to Waimea and then up to Kohala Mountain. It was another fine day, extremely clear and hot. The mountains were huge and seemed very close. "His ʻāina," he thought. He had lived on it for seventy-five years but wondered whether he would be able to finish the boy's training. There was still so much to teach him. However, a more pressing issue plagued Kaʻōkaʻi, would he be able to make the difficult climb as the party ascended the ever-increasing temperature-decreasing trail to the mountain? He need not have worried for the boy was always by his side.

They replenished their huewai dipping the gourds into Waiʻaka stream—fresh and cold from the mountain and clear from its filtering rocks. It fed the kalo fields at Puʻu Pā on its way down to the sea. Kaʻōkaʻi took a long draught and ate some dried ʻōpelu and pieces of dried poi. He felt better. They arrived at his younger sister's hale above Waimea's dry kalo fields and were grateful for a night's rest. Her husband and others would accompany the party into the forest where it was said some good-sized koa trees were growing above Waipiʻo and Waimanu Valleys.

The trees were not the first order of business that night however. There was excited talk of the recent battle at Mokuʻōhai and events leading up to it. Some of the men in the hale mua had just returned. They were part of Kamehameha's elite fighting force, the Kīpuʻupuʻu warriors of Waimea under their ali'i Keohuhu. This man's son Kailio, leader of the bow-men, was one of the men in the hale that night. The spears and fighting techniques of the Kīpu'upu'u were renowned. Great fighting men from the Kohala and Kona districts had also been part of the battle and talk was that Kamehameha was soon to be the king over all the islands. The story was told.

Kalani'ōpu'u, the supreme chief of Hawai'i Island, was close to death and had chosen his son Kīwala'ō as his heir. However, instead of giving the war god Kūkā'ilimoku and guardianship of all heiau to him, which would have been standard practice, Kalani'ōpu'u gave the god to Kamehameha with its accompanying heiau duties. What an insult!

When Kīwala'ō became king, he met with his loyal chiefs at Hōnaunau to apportion the island among them, but that did not please his half-brother, fiery and impetuous Keōua Kū'ahu'ula. What an insult!

Their uncle, greedy Keawemauhili of Hilo, received most of the gift lands. Keōua Kū'ahu'ula received none. What an insult!

Enraged, Keōua Kū'ahu'ula cut down coconut trees at Keomo, which was tantamount to murder and killed some of Kamehameha's warriors surfing at Ke'ei. What an insult!

Kīwala'ō accepted responsibility for his brother's declaration of war, and Kamehameha was forced into a contest. Kamehameha willingly challenged the sons of Kalani'ōpu'u. The place of Moku'ōhai was chosen by Kekūhaupi'o, Kamehameha's warrior-trainer. It was south of Kealakekua Bay from Ke'ei down to Hōnaunau. The ground was uneven and strewn with broken lava rock debris. Kekūhaupi'o knew it like the back of his hand. He grew up there and trained there and chose it for the advantage of Kamehameha's fighting men.

The opposing forces moved in from the south. Kamehameha's loyalists moved down from their assembly point at Nāpo'opo'o and Ke'ei led by Kekūhaupi'o over that very unstable battle-ground. Combat began in earnest. Ihe and pololū, short and long spears, raked the air and their points found flesh. Jagged shark-toothed weaponry bristling in the hands of the combatants took their toll on the bare-skinned warriors. Newa crushed skulls, and pāhoa cut into skin, and all manner of fighting implements and strategies crushed the foe. In the heat of battle, Kīwala'ō was hit in the temple by a stone thrown by an unknown assailant and collapsed on the field. At the same time, one of Kamehameha's loyal chiefs, Ke'eaumoku, was wounded by a spear. His half-brothers, the sacred twins Kamanawa and Kame'eiamoku, saw their brother fall and ran to his side along with a group of warriors. Ke'eaumoku managed to recover enough to move to the side of the injured Kīwala'ō and killed him with a lei o manō. Kamehameha's opposition fled at the death of their king.

'Eleu had been listening intently to the men recently in the throes of battle, but his little black eyes were beginning to get very heavy. Then he heard something that caused him to bolt upright. His eyes caught Ka'ōka'i's eyes in the half-light. The men were talking about a fearless warrior who excelled in the art of lua and who, it was said, was almost as good as Kekūhaupi'o. His name was Kanewa, and he was the cause of many of Kamehameha's men to die on that battlefield. Ka'ōka'i shook his head to warn 'Eleu not to say a word.

The discussion suddenly turned to stories of great-sized koa trees made into wonderful canoes for the ali'i. The great Waimea warriors were not canoe-men, but they knew their wood especially the kauila saplings used for their spears—strong, dense, holding a point. Koa was also used as were other woods of ka nahele, the forest. They knew where those specific trees were.

While the 'awa cup was passed around, 'Eleu's ears perked up when someone mentioned the huge tree trunks washed up on Kaua'i's and Ni'ihau's northeast shores. Unknown logs of very large proportions made into extremely fine canoes were famous in all the islands. Someone said they were from some place called the Pacific Northwest Coast. "What a strange name," thought 'Eleu. Another said that logs had floated to Ka'ū at Kamilo where its swirling currents captured logs and other flotsam into the small inlet. That night, 'Eleu's dreams were filled with questions about swimming logs.

The next morning, ground fog covered the grasses and clung to the kalo plants, allowing only the heart-shaped lau to be seen standing above the mist. 'Eleu woke up early, feeling the freezing cold under his kapa blanket, and he went outside the hale moe to see what he thought was another kapa covering the ground. When he began walking on it, he said out loud, "Where are my feet? And it's wet!" He ran in circles causing the mist to swirl around his legs. "What kind of spirit is this?" he thought. It disintegrated right before his eyes. He had never seen such a thing. 'Eleu had straggled off quite a distance before he heard the oli, and his heart sank as he headed back.

By the time the men finished their chanting to the family gods, 'Eleu discovered the reason for the 'ahu lā'ī, ti-leaf capes; it was cold! And while placing the cape on 'Eleu's shoulders, Ka'ōka'i chided him for missing the oli. "You must think, 'Eleu, of the traditions we do in our lives. They are for a purpose," he said forcefully. The boy remembered his father's stern words to him three years before. A dark cloud of guilt hung over the nine-year-old. Why couldn't he remember?

Thoughts of shame didn't last long for preparations began for the trek into the mountain. Trails were well-known by the warriors, and they headed for the pali areas above the

Waipi'o, Waimanu, and Pololū valleys, into the Mahiki forest. 'Eleu's eyes caught everything from leaf litter to treetops, from delicate red lehua blossoms to rough leather-like green leaves—some shiny and some dull with bark both smooth and rough. He began to notice shapes of different trees in the canopy, pointed out to him by his great-grandfather's soft voice.

The earthy smells, aromas, and fragrances of the dry dusty trail or the dank wetness of gulch crossings were beginning to whet his appetite. Those senses were new to him, and they were exciting.

On and on they walked. There was a māmane tree used to build hale; there an 'ōhi'a lehua whose root among other parts was used for strength in forming wae, the U-shaped braces in a canoe. 'Eleu touched the trunks, memorizing the surfaces. The ko'oko'olau or māmaki plants were used for tea and medicine. He broke off leaves, crushing and tasting them. Koali 'awa vines mixed with kō shoots and mashed with pa'akai fixed broken bones.

'Eleu's mind wandered when he remembered his young cousin's broken arm back in Kapa'ahu. Nāihe the kahuna lā'au lapa'au told the boy it would itch very much but not to touch the poultice no matter what. 'Eleu kept his cousin busy, finding the right kind of pebbles for playing kōnane (checkers) and kinikini (marbles) and challenging him to many games. Within three days, the bone was set.

Ka'ōka'i touched 'Eleu's shoulder to bring him back to the teaching at hand. "Did you know that kukui is not only used for light?" 'Eleu shook his head. "The flowers, leaves, bark and seeds are also useful for medicine. Here's an 'ōlena (turmeric) used for dyes and other medicines as well." 'Eleu remembered wistfully that his mother loved the yellow hue her sister used to decorate Kamahinaohōkū's kapa.

Ka'ōka'i said a little louder, "Pay attention, 'Eleu. 'Awapuhi is not just for fragrance for your hair or lei but for herbal treatment." 'Eleu lost part of the 'awapuhi discussion.

"Here's a hau tree." He cut a branch and began peeling it into thin strips; he told the boy that dry-land hau, which was stronger, was preferred for 'iako, the booms of the canoe. 'Eleu's eyes got very wide. He was learning canoe-making terms. "We use this for kaula," Ka'ōka'i said, handing him the strips. "Do you know another plant we use for cordage?" he asked.

"Niu," 'Eleu said definitively. "I saw my makua kāne roll the fibers on his thigh and make many little cords and very large ones."

"That is excellent, 'Eleu. Your father was very good at all aspects of canoe-making. Another type of kaula is made with 'ākia."

'Eleu felt proud, and just maybe the old respect for his father was beginning to return. And he was proud of himself that he had been paying attention to important things after all.

Suddenly, 'Eleu felt strange. "My kupuna kuakahi, I am afraid!" He pulled close to the old man. "There is a strange power all around me."

Ka'ōka'i smiled and said it was his birthright to feel such things. "It is the mana in the forest you feel, little one. There are many forces here in this place. Our ancestors began right down there in Waipi'o Valley. They landed on that beach from our ancient place of beginning—Hawaiki." He directed 'Eleu's gaze down into the valley. "Many of our ancestors lived and died in these areas. We will paddle there someday soon when we make our wa'a."

Immediately, there was a rush of activity and many voices. Numerous useful saplings and small-size koa trees were scattered along the trail, but off into a kula mau'u, a grassy meadow, there it stood—a koa of enormous proportions and perfectly straight. The voices were quiet. 'Eleu was astounded as he craned his neck skyward.

A kahuna kālai wa'a from Kailua's Kealakōwa'a heiau and a friend of Ka'ōka'i's brother-in-law had been invited on the trip to examine the tree, making sure it was sound and to perform the ritual ceremonies. At the base of the tree, the canoe builder expert began the prayers invoking Lea, the goddess of canoe builders. He carried a pua'a hiwa, the black pig, a red fish, and a red kapa garment as an offering. The red fish and kapa were buried at the base of the tree with a bunch of kohekohe sedge, and the pig would be baked in the imu.

A suitable spot was chosen to dig the pit to roast the pua'a. Some men attended to that task; others including 'Eleu and his great-grandfather began gathering the wood and thatch for temporary shelters. They would be in the forest for some time.

'Eleu was learning how to use his adze expertly on the saplings. He would graduate to larger trees as his training progressed.

The warriors went back to Waimea to leave the felling of the big tree to the experts. Their guidance into the forest was done, but they would come back with many more hands—men, women, and children—to move the partially completed canoe to its final destination for finishing. All offerings, prayers, and ceremonial eating were accomplished, and everything was ready.

Smaller trees were removed so the koa would not collide with them and break. Also, the placement of the largest branch on the tree was noted so it would fall onto that cushion. Hāpu'u fern, both stump and fronds, were cut to further cushion it. Dirt was dug away from the roots so the bottom would not split, and many men began cutting those roots. If the gods were with them, it would not split.

Some minor cracking was heard, and the tree began to sway. Everyone jumped back, and it fell right onto its cushion. A cloud of dust and leaves filtered through the forest air, and the felled tree gave a great thump. The priest and men ran to the upturned root system and examined it. Any remaining roots were removed. The trunk was sound! It was not split! Glorious oli from priests' powerful voices resonated through the wooded forest thanking Lea.

"Watch the 'elepaio, 'Eleu," Ka'ōka'i said softly. "It will tell us if the tree is good." There was no food for that bird, and it flew away. The men looked at each other and smiled. They went to sleep that night in their lean-to shelters, satisfied that that stage of the work was complete. The next day, the hewing of the log would begin.

In the morning, the kapu was satisfied with prayers by the kahuna, and the tree's crown was cut off. Adzes began their work as the men wielding them removed bark and interior wood. Thudding sounds of basalt striking solid log reverberated throughout the forest. The work brought the log to a state for its transportation. 'Umi'umi hauling ropes were attached to the back end of the log to secure the rough-shaped canoe. Kaula kūpe'e, tethering ropes, would restrain it on the downhill trail to Kawaihae. With so many hands, including the men from Waimea who had returned, processes that would have taken months took much less time.

'Eleu thought about his ancestors doing this work over the centuries. He was keenly aware of his heritage, his 'āina, his place in the scheme of things. He watched. He learned. He acknowledged the wealth of survival skills from his great-grandfather and all those men. He also remembered his father and the loving care placed on every canoe he would ever make. 'Eleu resolved he would always honor the man who gave him life, and his tender heart remembered his beautiful mother whom he would never forget.

PĀ – LUA SCHOOL

One fine morning in 1788, 'Eleu and Wai'aha were out fishing not far from shore in one of the small canoes they made. It was carved beautifully, and they were very proud of it. Both had become fine canoe makers and took pride in making them for others.

As they started back in, someone was frantically motioning to them from the beach. Shading his eyes, Wai'aha began to wave back but discovered it was not friendly waving. Kuluwaimaka, one of Ka'ōka'i's oldest friends, said to the boys as they beached the canoe, "Hurry! The old man is sick." They ran all the way to his ma uka home above Honokoa at Waipāhoehoe stream.

The signs had been there all along, but Ka'ōka'i again and again denied that anything was wrong. 'Eleu had found him several times over the course of the last few months either bent over clutching his chest or rubbing his left arm, but the pain always subsided. He was resting, watching 'Eleu prepare the fish caught for their dinner. He was proud of the boy. At fifteen, 'Eleu was beginning to show good muscle tone. Wai'aha stayed with them instead of going back to his own hale. Ka'ōka'i noted how much Wai'aha had grown into a tall, well-muscled, and handsome young man in the yellow malo. It was said many girls were glancing his way. He was a close companion to 'Eleu, treating him like a younger brother. The two had become inseparable.

"E 'Eleu ē," Ka'ōka'i said barely above a whisper, "you have learned very much from me since you came into my home. Your skills are numerous especially making beautiful canoes. I've tried to give you the knowledge of your ancestors so you may make your way in the world, but I think my time with you is coming to an end. There is one more trip I want to make with you though. You need to learn the art of lua.

A man must learn how to defend himself and use the implements we have for our defense. Wai'aha, will you travel with us to Ke'ei? I have talked to Kuluwaimaka, who as you know was a great warrior in his younger years. He feels the time is right for the boy and has received word from that famous camp of his admittance to the school of Kekūhaupi'o."

'Eleu's emotions were in turmoil, being both stunned that he would not be with his great-grandfather anymore and pleased to be learning the warriors' arts. He had been secretly practicing moves he saw some of the local warriors doing. He began to protest though as he did not want to leave Ka'ōka'i. The old man sensed the boy was distressed but told 'Eleu that all things must come to an end.

Ka'ōka'i would not be making the trip after all.

He closed his eyes on a sunset that was staggering in its brilliant beauty. Golden hues bathed his glorious 'āina as he looked from mountain to sea. Mauna Kea, Mauna Loa, and Hualālai were wreathed in coral and gray lei po'o and bathed with the reddish-brown color of cinder and the red of royal feather robe. Darkest black spread out from mountain recesses like thieves snatching away the land. Bands of clouds pressed on by breezes stretched across the sky, changing from coral to gray then disappearing in whispers of mists. Water and sky in color of kai uli, the deep blue sea, disappeared with the final rays of the sun on the horizon. The world for Ka'ōka'i had come to an end with a prayer on his lips to his Ma'iola, god of healing. His spirit, 'uhane, would enter its next phase of existence. He would be off to the ao 'aumākua, the world of his family gods.

As Kuluwaimaka chanted an uwē kanikau, a dirge of mourning, telling of Ka'ōka'i's life and the aloha he had, he helped 'Eleu prepare the body of the venerable great-grandfather for burial. The bundle of his bones was quietly set into a burial cave at Honokoa. When they returned to Ka'ōka'i's home, Kuluwaimaka blessed each of them with kai, the salt-water, to be cleansed of the dead spirit. They then prepared a meal for themselves.

It seemed as if 'Eleu was always leaving behind the known for the unknown. His mind was a confusion of uncertainties. He knew what was important in life, but why were those things always snatched away from him?

Submerging those thoughts in the task at hand, the boy-turning-to-man grabbed the paddle, touched its 'upe to the surface then sank the blade deep in the water and pulled the canoe forward with his friends. Kuluwaimaka would introduce 'Eleu into the world of lua, but for that moment, 'Eleu's only thought would be the present moment of wood canoe, bright blue water, and the spray-drenched bodies of the young man and the old man escorting him to his future.

In his mind, 'Eleu waved good-bye to his second home and felt Ka'ōka'i turn his head again to the future as he had done so many times before. 'Eleu smiled. "Eō, e ku'u kupuna kuakahi! Yes, my great-grandfather, I am listening!"

Forty-five miles to the south was Kealakekua Bay and their destination, Ke'ei, the camp of the illustrious Kekūhaupi'o. 'Eleu and Wai'aha were invited to dinner with the younger students that night. Kuluwaimaka would join the instructors as the aged lua warrior of many battles was well-known.

In the cool of the morning, before the weather changed to a scorching day, the new students were escorted around the Pā by the master, an 'ōlohe lua. Their attention was drawn to every facet of the mock battles going on around them and the repetitious practice with battle weapons.

Kuluwaimaka went with the group enjoying his memories of when he learned the great arts of lua tactics with La'amea, one of Kekūhaupi'o's kumu.

Wai'aha, however, preferred busying himself with off-loading 'Eleu's things into the hale he would be sharing with his peers. The twenty-year-old did not have the inclination to acquire such knowledge, preferring to grapple with a koa log instead of another human being. He refilled the 'olowai, their canoe water gourds, for the return trip. Soon, the two men would be off, leaving 'Eleu to himself in his new surroundings. 'Eleu swallowed the urge to cry when they finally departed. They were his friends, and he steeled himself to yet another loss. The new course of action would make him or crush him—his choice. He decided he would not be crushed.

"You will sweat, 'Eleu," the instructor growled at him as if trying to discourage his new young student.

'Eleu was not put off for during his days of canoe-making work, he was hot and sweaty from beginning to end. He started to defend himself but quickly noticed a challenging glance. He was learning fast.

Tauntingly, the instructor again growled, squeezing 'Eleu's upper arms, "I see you have some fine muscles sprouting there. Been chasing girls, boy?"

'Eleu gritted his teeth. It was turning into a contest of wills. Or was it? A thought occurred to him, "That's the point, nothing should get to you."

'Eleu was sized up by his instructor. He was a little tall for his age. "Hmm, a bit lanky and likely to grow taller since he is only fifteen," the man thought as he circled the boy. "Should have started last year, the ideal age. More pliable," he mumbled.

"What?" 'Eleu questioned.

"Nothing," the man said louder, cutting the boy a little slack as he knew 'Eleu had been raised by Ka'ōka'i, the respected kahuna lā'au lapa'au known even that far south. The instructor knew something else about 'Eleu that

Kuluwaimaka had shared when they first arrived—information that was not shared in the hale mua at Waimea.

Six years earlier, 'Eleu's father Kanewa had been a ferocious fighter on the side of Kamehameha's enemies at the Battle of Moku'ōhai just south of the lua school. The instructor had seen the man and was impressed by his fearlessness. Whether that would work to 'Eleu's favor or not, he would have to see as Kanewa had been a foe to the men in the lua camp.

"Kekūhaupi'o is shorter and stockier. That's also ideal. Like a log, not a coconut tree." 'Eleu didn't know what the instructor was talking about. He was what he was, not what should have been. He passed off the remark as not worthy of thought. That was good advice to himself which he would remember. He heard the instructor say, "One day when you graduate, you will be known as warrior, a koa. For now, you are a haumāna, one of the students."

The haumāna were sent upslope of Hōnaunau to look for the proper plants to adorn the altar of the Pā. Lazy boys, disliking the cold, simply wanted to get back to the warmth of the shore. They hurried through their oli and only took the abundant maile, a fragrant twining plant. 'Eleu, however, wanted more and went farther than the others.

He remembered when his parents first brought him at five years old to Hōnaunau to visit Kanewa's family. While there on a hunting party for wauke, māmane, ma'aloa, and the flesh of the fern shoot—the pala holo—to make kapa, 'Eleu's grandmother Aweola'akea had pointed out a rare white lehua puakea, a white-blossomed 'ōhi'a tree. That day the boy's curious attention was only given to crawly things on the ground.

Venturing higher and thoroughly annoying the others, he finally found the lehua puakea. With his hands on the tree and bowing his head, he asked Pele humbly for permission to cut the branches that would highlight the Pā's altar.

As the newest member of the haumāna, 'Eleu stood at the entrance of the Pā to be received by the kanaka kālī kukui, the man in charge of the kukui torches, and the kia'i puka, guard of the door. He gave the proper password when asked. And with pride in his ancestry, his arms and body movements punctuating the significance of words and phrases of the oli, he implored all the gods of the lua to bless him and give him the strength he needed to complete his training. His rich bass voice with full vibrato, practiced through his canoe-making days, rang out over the whole assembly stopping them in their tracks. 'Eleu then produced the lovely white blossomed lehua puakea branches from his basket and presented them to the 'ōlohe lua with many nods of approval.

Their daily schedule was always the same after the morning meal; warm-up stretches and exercise designed to prevent injuries were required of all would-be warrior-trainees. Running until 'Eleu thought his lungs would collapse seemed to be another daily test to see if he would give up. He endured. Always, new chants had to be learned, and passwords that changed daily would allow admission to the Pā each day. If one forgot the password or neglected those chants, he was out of the school. Parts of the body were to be recited without hesitation. Proper stance was taught for balance. Methods of punching, kicking, and blocking were practiced from dawn to dusk with ever increasing strength and stamina. 'Eleu noticed that many sham battles were worked on at night. He knew that some techniques were kept secret, and he wondered about those maneuvers.

From time to time, visiting Pā would come to challenge the advanced students so as not to get stale, and 'Eleu and the other haumāna would be able to watch and learn how the different techniques were put into practice. They watched and learned successful and not so successful ways to do things as evidenced by those who made mistakes and were put down and humiliated.

In February 1789, 'Eleu turned sixteen and felt he was doing quite well. A Kohala Pā, those Kīpu'upu'u spear experts he knew first hand, came to challenge Kekūhaupi'o's men. 'Eleu was asked to be part of the exercises for the day by the 'ōlohe lua. His ego was rejoicing, but his faint heart felt a tug of panic as Kekūhaupi'o himself would be there to observe not only the students but the masters themselves. Pololū throwing and fighting using that long spear was not his strength. He was taller by a couple of inches but found that implement to be unwieldy. He much preferred the short spear, hand implements, and especially the pīkoi to trip up all contenders, his favorite.

The day of fame or infamy came, and individuals and groups were chosen to square off. Spear throwing at targets was the first game. 'Eleu could barely hit the side of a hale let alone the middle of a small target but decided to have fun with the sport and give it his best shot. "Not bad," he thought as he hit the side of the target nowhere close to center. He received frowns for his effort from the 'ōlohe lua and snickers and taunts from the men of the Kohala side.

Close-in contact with the spear was next. At one point, 'Eleu tripped over the end of the spear when he fought with a boy about his same age. The action only brought laughter even from his own side. He gave up and decided it was no use at all. He'd wait for the next challenge.

It came—hand-to-hand combat. 'Eleu took his stance across from a big strapping fellow twice as heavy as he was. He gulped. Suddenly, the boy lunged at him, but 'Eleu saw it coming. Being pretty fast, he neatly stepped aside and used the momentum to push the boy down in the dirt. In a flash, the boy was up, and 'Eleu, who was not properly seated in his stance, was surprised by a punch that grazed his chin. 'Eleu reeled a little, realizing that if the boy had found his target, he would be out cold on the ground. More punches were exchanged as were some ineffective leg sweeps designed to trip the opponent. A mighty right punch was launched by the visiting boy. From his waist, 'Eleu rotated his left arm up and across, palm and fingers outstretched, blocking the boy's elongated punch. He kept the rotation going, came up under the upper arm, grabbed and pulled it toward him, and stepped in with a right knuckle punch landing on his jaw. The boy fell at 'Eleu's feet unconscious. He stepped back feeling redeemed, a victor to the cheering crowds.

'Eleu had perfected his pīkoi throwing to such an extent that his reputation in the Pā was unsurpassed. He practiced day and night at odd moments, constantly testing stones and wood for weights and lengths and types of olonā or hau cordage for strength until he was satisfied that his own style of weapon could become an extension of either hand. He tripped up many a man from the Kohala Pā.

Graduation was upon them, but Kekūhaupiʻo would not be at the ceremony. He was on Maui with his liege lord Kamehameha in a fight with King Kalanikūpule for domination of the island. The Battle of Kepaniwai, the dammed waters of ʻĪao Valley, was decisive for the Aliʻi Kamehameha, but there was much carnage on both sides. The king wanted Oʻahu next but had to return to Hawaiʻi Island to fight the thorn in his side, Keōua Kūʻahuʻula. He was the last independent chief there and was again trying to devour ground already won by a man he would not accept as king.

By the time Kekūhaupiʻo returned, ʻEleu had been teaching in the Pā. The master was back from the victory at Maui, gathering his trained elite warriors and prepared to meet with Kamehameha in Kohala. He watched with the ʻōlohe lua ʻEleu's teaching techniques.

"What do you think of this young man?" Kekūhaupiʻo asked the teacher.

"He will be great someday," the instructor answered. "His lineage is problematic though, but his strengths are secure."

"I see his strengths. What is this problematic lineage you speak about?"

"His father fought the king and you at Mokuʻōhai. During the battle, I saw his skills as a lua fighter, and they reminded me of the techniques of the great Laʻamea."

Kekūhaupiʻo was startled at the instructor's comparison of his own teacher causing him to sift through his student days. "What is this enemy's name?"

"Kanewa. It was discovered that he was under the Puna district chief in charge of caring for the royal lands from the luakini heiau of Wahaʻula to Kaimū. His ancestry is cloudy.

Nothing in the oli speaks of him, but he seems to be a chief. It appears he might have been the next district chief had it not been for his wife's death. After which, he threw himself into many battles. His canoe-making skills were extraordinary and highly sought after by Kalaniʻōpuʻu. ʻEleu is his son but raised by the kahuna Kaʻōkaʻi, learning many arts, not the least of which are his exquisite canoe-making skills like his father."

Kekūhaupiʻo raised an eyebrow, deliberating. Slowly, he said, "I want ʻEleu for the king's battle with that kolohe Keōua. Put him in my canoe. We'll see what he can do."

Over the next year, ʻEleu would be tested in the fights of the battles of Eastern Hawaiʻi, and Keōua would be beaten back at each incursion at Laupāhoehoe, Hakalau, and the water battle at Waipiʻo. He was rewarded with leadership of a forty-man division and was present at Kawaihae when Keōua was "requested" to be present at the dedication of the newly constructed luakini heiau of Puʻukoholā. In that year of 1791, Keōua Kūʻahuʻula became its first sacrifice and would trouble "his king" no more.

ʻEleu was elevated to an ʻōlohe lua at Kekūhaupiʻo's great school and continued to live in Keʻei for the next four years.

BATTLE OF NUʻUANU PALI

In May 1795, thousands of canoes covered the shores and landing places along six miles of Oʻahu's south shore. No sand or rocky coast was seen from Waiʻalae to Waikīkī. ʻEleu was leading a forty-man division of Kamehameha's forces, and all his men surrounded him in their canoes. A wide deserted ʻāina was between them and the Koʻolau Mountain range as aliʻi and makaʻāinana alike either hid at some far distant place or had joined forces with Oʻahu's defending King

Kalanikūpule. For three days in preparation on both sides, the gods were plied with prayers and offerings for victory.

'Eleu tied his malo flap securely at his waist. He then wrapped the protective lauhala mat around his middle, fastening it with a band of kapa, the pāhoa held tightly between the layers. Tied over the kapa was his pīkoi to be easily freed when the time came. He and his men smeared their bodies with oil.

Kamehameha, with his warrior Kekūhaupi'o by his side, led his army in the first skirmishes at the heiau behind Pūowaina[4], the bowl-like crater. Kalanikūpule's warriors were then pushed back to their next fortified position at La'imi Heiau. It was blasted away by Kamehameha's artillery. In the smoke and confusion, Kalanikūpule's forces continued to be beaten back, fighting as they retreated to Pu'iwa then to Ahipu'u Heiau then finally to the cliffs above Nu'uanu Valley.

'Eleu with newa pōhaku in hand led his men through the thick foliage. The wedge-shaped formation quickly fell apart in the difficult terrain. An enemy tried to grab hold of his too-slippery target and was slashed in the groin for his effort. Another clawed at 'Eleu's head but only had a greased palm and broken skull for his trouble. 'Eleu's long hair, plucked out weeks before the battle, was as short as it had been when he was a child.

'Eleu led his koa over the ridge in front of them. Suddenly, a large contingent of the enemy came up from the other side. It would be face-to-face and hand-to-hand combat. They looked into each other's eyes not more than a few yards away. Many warriors gave blood-curdling cries. Some made themselves puffed up so they would seem larger and more frightening foes and give themselves courage. Shouted

---

4.   Punch Bowl

enticements of derogatory exclamations egged on the combatants. Within seconds, the battle began in earnest with enemy spears whistling through the smoky air. Thuds of cannon balls from the white men's guns, thuds of newa on skulls, and the cracks of backs broken across knees were like the horrible beat of pahu on the battlefield. Warriors using strangling cords quickly dispatched their opponents, and shark-tooth weapons caused blood to run down on to the uneven terrain and into the swirling dust.

'Eleu took down some men directly in front of him, using his newa to pound heads. As he pulled out his pāhoa from the folds of his waist's binding, enemy eyes did not see the stealthy movement. The fingers of his right hand grasped the weapon securely, and then the pāhoa was unrecoverable in the ribcage of a man directly to the right. He fell. Two others took his place, and with swift moves, 'Eleu put both men down before either suspected they were about to die.

Suddenly, a frightening seven-foot warrior stepped before him, spewing epithets from his gaping mouth, spit of Ps and Ts of the ancient language punctuating the air. 'Eleu swallowed hard, not showing his fear. He knew height might not be an advantage for the man. In a split second, he went low, his mat deflecting a death-dealing pāhoa blow from the enemy towering over him, and with all his might, he threw his body at the man's knees. At the same instant, 'Eleu's friend got behind, drawing the unstable enemy warrior backward, his fist breaking the man's back. Their training together paid off, and a well-done nod was shared.

Behind the contingent, 'Eleu was aware of a man coming fast toward him. He was a savage-looking warrior, battle scarred and completely fearless. A bloody red and yellow feather kīpuka covered his right shoulder. His hair was loose on one side, flying around his head and shoulders but partially matted on the other, from a blow already received.

'Eleu as a lua koa trained to use both hands equally well. He remembered thinking to himself that the man was left-handed and that hand held a terrible looking lipi hoehoe, the broad paddle-like adze surrounded by shark teeth dripping with blood. He was coming directly for 'Eleu, who the warrior recognized as the leader and worthy of death.

'Eleu wasted no time and freed his pīkoi from around his waist and threw the stone weight of it with his right hand at the approaching warrior. It caught, and the man fell directly at 'Eleu's feet. The only weapon remaining was the newa dangling from his left wrist. He raised the implement to crush the man's skull just as the warrior lifted himself up and looked directly at 'Eleu. Despite the stains of dirt and blood on both men's faces, there was an instant of recognition. The warrior was his own father, Kanewa. "The war club!" At that moment, 'Eleu's friend, coming to his aid again, speared that enemy in his back. 'Eleu's face was full of terror. His friend's face was full of bewilderment, and his father's face was filled with agony.

"My makua kāne," 'Eleu wailed, dropping to his knees.

With Kanewa's last painful breath and a weak smile he whispered, "E ku'u lei ē." There was a surprising look of love and pride in that twisted face scarred from many battles, physical as well as mental. Kanewa, calling 'Eleu "my beloved child," died in his own son's arms.

It was only then that with the kīpuka parted 'Eleu saw a lei niho palaoa around his father's neck. The whale tooth was broken but still clinging to the human-hair lei. 'Eleu was stunned. Why was his father wearing the lei of an ali'i?

The battle continued with Kalanikūpule escaping with his wounds. Many retreated along old trails. Most had been killed. The remainder, pushed to the edges of the one-thousand-foot pali, chose to jump, and eight hundred skulls would be found at the base at some future time. 'Eleu's blood-stained mat from a wound in his side was ragged from blows and had done its work protecting him.

The gods looked kindly on Kamehameha who had destroyed the armies of Kalanikūpule. And the people looked kindly on Kamehameha after the battle when he let go the captives and employed kāhuna lapa'au to tend to the wounded. The people found their dead for burial, and the stunned Ali'i Nui found many disheveled kalo fields. The people would not be able to eat to live! The king began to rebuild those lo'i using his own hands, his warriors, and the O'ahu maka'āinana to repair and then to replant the huli.

Kamehameha went around the island using the people from each village to join him in the restoration of their planted fields. He noted destroyed fish ponds and desired that they be rebuilt, so he began assembling the rocks himself. Everyone returned to repairing their beloved 'āina. It took nearly one year to complete the circuit and bring Oʻahu to its former glory.

Following their king, many of Kamehameha's koa found the villages of Oʻahu pleasant and decided to stay. When they reached Waimānalo, ʻEleu found it a beautiful place and lush with vegetation, and having no one to return to on Hawaiʻi Island, he wanted to make a fresh start. Kamehameha's intention after the Oʻahu defeat was to bring Kauaʻi under his reign, but circumstances were against him. A messenger brought him news of a rebellion at home.

SETTLING IN WAIMĀNALO (1796)

ʻEleu was twenty-three years old and was accepted by the local villagers when the fear of him as conqueror wore off. He slept outside in the elements and worked hard for the people. He became a builder in the eyes of the makaʻāinana, not a destroyer, and he was esteemed by them with the blood and bones of his father mingling with those of the defeated Oʻahu people. After months of ʻāina rescue, happiness and regularity returned, and the people helped ʻEleu build his own hale—gathering supports, tying with ʻaha (cord braided of coconut husk), thatching with pili grass—slow work for one man but done in no time with many hands.

To celebrate, a puaʻa was roasted in the imu along with moa and ʻuala. Thick starchy poi was deliciously licked from fingers along with juicy ʻaʻama. Crunchy ʻōhiʻa ʻai, soft spoon meat of the coconut along with its refreshing water was thoroughly enjoyed by everyone including puppies licking wayward drops of broth from the ʻōpū in the laps of their masters.

On evenings before the light vanished from the land, ʻEleu would enjoy a climb up the slope behind his hale to feel the cool makani and watch it brush the kalo's heart-shaped lau. Freshwater mullet moved their silvery bodies in and out of the loʻi. It was a good place. Stands of maiʻa and ʻulu were everywhere. Niu and kō dotted the landscape. He could see the Kaʻelepulu pond in Kailua bathed in the evening twilight and so full of fish. All those things sustained life. It was a very good place.

ʻEleu thought he would miss the battles. He'd been at them for six years, but a period of peace settled over the land with the great Kamehameha as aliʻi nui over most all the islands.

But there was another longing in the heart of the canoe maker's son; something was missing in his life. Still buried down deep was the desire to sail on a ship. Or maybe it was his desire to build canoes, his first love. Or maybe it was a woman and children he needed. In the end, loneliness had come to call, but his circumstances at the moment determined his course.

One day, after he had been in Waimānalo a little over a year, a different call came from an old kupuna who lived nearby. In the evening, the two would sit and talk, sharing stories and ʻawa by kukui nut torch, their shadowy figures reflected on the hale behind them. ʻEleu was reminded of the great-grandfather Kaʻōkaʻi he loved so much a long time ago. The man's dark face was full of wisdom, craggy like the Koʻolau mountains, a broad flat nose and long gray hair pulled back with ʻaha cord. By ʻEleu's calculations, the man was at least in his eighties as he remembered the ancient Oʻahu kings. ʻEleu knew some of the oli sung about those men the old man mentioned. The two men—one young and one old—became fast friends.

Another day, ʻEleu had been repairing a broken rock wall behind the old man's hale and came around the corner to behold a stunningly beautiful girl. A great-granddaughter was bringing her great-grandfather ʻuala and poi, roast pig, and dried fish from their family as she did several times a month. A fragrant white hibiscus behind each ear held long brown-black wavy hair. A kīhei covered her torso and a pāʻū skirt modestly hid her virtues. She was tall and well built, a good-sized girl and a little over half his age.

He immediately forgot about building the wall. Sweat ran in rivulets through the dirt he wore from head to toe, giving him a ghastly appearance. His malo was torn to pieces by the jagged rocks, and his pū, the knot of hair on his head, was completely lopsided, wayward strands flying everywhere. The girl turned and was terrified by the ferocious ghost before her and ran to her great-grandfather for protection. The old man laughed when he saw ʻEleu grin sheepishly. No wonder she was frightened.

Kahikina was her name. She averted her eyes when her great-grandfather introduced her to ʻEleu. "What manner of man was this covered with lepo?" she thought. The great-grandfather was asking him to share their meal? What an insult! The old man convinced her to wait patiently. After a little while as the girl shared news of the family in Kailua, ʻEleu returned a new man, and she saw how handsome he was.

"You look better clean," she said, teasing him.

"E kala mai iaʻu for my appearance," ʻEleu said apologetically.

He wore a clean malo for a start and stood there in her presence at six feet four inches. His shiny wet hair was pulled back in a neat pū which enhanced his clear brown skin like highly polished koa. With a wide forehead, a brow strong and proud, a broad nose, a big happy smile, and sparkling black eyes, what more could a girl ask?

Kahikina sighed. Of course, there were those big shoulders covered with tattoos down to the elbows. She knew they were from his lua-training days as the great-grandfather had related to her while awaiting 'Eleu's return. Those intricate patterns moved about on very large muscles in the afternoon sun as he engaged in lively conversation.

Kahikina was smitten. 'Eleu was smitten. What then?

Unfortunately, Kahikina had to leave them as she had a long walk back to Kailua, and the day was waning. 'Eleu didn't see her for a while, but she left a call of longing in his heart that replaced the loneliness. He vowed to fix that situation.

Relief did not come until a few months later. 'Eleu went fishing with a friend in his canoe, and the canoe maker's son paid him a compliment about the sturdy construction of the craft. He did not want to be nīele or rude about its maker. It floated and that was all that counted. The friend as it turned out was not the maker and had received the canoe from a local builder living in Kailua. A spark of excitement hit 'Eleu. The friend was going to get a fine catch to add to the price already set for the canoe. 'Eleu's heart skipped a beat as they would take the catch to Kailua that day! The fishing gods were with them, and they made a fine haul. When they beached the canoe later in the day, the maker met them smiling broadly over the work of his hands and the great quantity of fish it contained. 'Eleu remembered the fine highly polished canoes he had made years ago and the superb quality of the double-hulled wa'a produced by his father and requested by ali'i, but he decided to say nothing. Instead, he pitched in to help his friend and the crowd bring in the fish. 'Eleu was invited to their feast that evening.

Oh, joy! There was Kahikina in her glory. Her kapa pā'ū skirt was decorated with colorful intricate designs and tied up and about her hips. Kahikina was in the line of hula dancers, the entertainment for the evening. She was with the unmarried girls with their long hair. He noted hers did not cover her topless torso. The other women of the troupe had the short style, hair bleached white in front, common to their child-bearing status. Fragrant flowers and ferns decorated their bodies, and lei poʻo of shells and seeds were worn on their heads. ʻEleu's heart was in his throat, and he was barely able to speak.

The kumu hula said, "Kū!" and the women stood erect with hands on hips. "Hoʻomākaukau." The make-ready signal was given.

The musicians beat out the introduction in measured rhythms by slapping ipu heke ʻole, the bottle gourd with no top, and beating of pahu hula (drum) with the dancers following closely the words of the oli in their leg and arm movements.

The first was a luna, or standing hula, with knees bent low and hips kaʻo (swaying) or ʻami (circling) ʻākau and hema, right and left. It was so sensual with ʻuwehe, knees lifting and separating and so flirtatious. All movements were seductive to honor Aliʻi Nui Kamehameha.

There was a hula noho for the birthday of the recently installed aliʻi of Oʻahu put in place by the great king himself. That chant was in praise of his genitals called mele maʻi using the swish-rattle of feathered ʻulīʻulī in the left hand with the right hand communicating the words. The throbbing of the rhythms, the intoxicating fragrances, and the dancers' movements made ʻEleu's head swim. He could not look away; he could not eat. The entertainment went on for hours, and ʻEleu blotted out everything but his Kahikina. He was in love.

Staying the night with the men of Kahikina's family and sharing their ʻawa, ʻEleu was the butt of their jokes for most of the evening. He was a bit embarrassed, but he had done the same things to others, so he did not mind the fun. It was the men's ways. In the morning when all the meal proprieties were accomplished, he greeted Kahikina's father in friendship.

"Aloha kāua, I wish to speak with you about certain items of importance."

The older man smiled. He knew the young man had a fine reputation and was pleased to finally meet him as his daughter drove everyone hoʻopupule with the talk of him.

ʻEleu pressed on. "It's regarding Kahikina's great-grandfather." The man gasped in fear. This was his grandfather the young man was talking about.

"Is he all right?" he asked. "I know you have been helping him."

"Yes, but I fear his weakness has become worse over the last few weeks. I have been planting and repairing for him, and the villagers have been helping him sustain life. I understand Kahikina has been bringing food for some time."

"She's a good girl," the man said softly. "But he's paʻakikī as you probably know. He and my kūkū wahine (grandmother) would not leave Waimānalo Ahupuaʻa when we moved here. We had trouble with the konohiki (headman). Kailua, no pilikia (trouble). Kūkū died last year, but he wouldn't budge. Kahikina keeps an eye out for him."

"I agree he is stubborn...and I have a proposition for you..." He paused for breath. "If I could hoʻāo your daughter, I would love her and take care of her...and my care would extend to her great-grandfather...and mākuahūnōai, my new in-law ʻohana."

Kahikina's father was pleased and without words that the man was proposing a change of the old ways. Normally when a man married a woman, he would move to her homestead. Instead, he was offering a kindness, a satisfactory solution to the problem.

"Wait here?" he asked. "I will speak to the family and my daughter."

'Eleu sat at the door of the hale mua. He wondered if he would be accepted by both Kahikina and her 'ohana. The minutes hung in the air expectantly. "What would be the outcome? Would they accept me? Would she accept me?" He would let his 'aumākua decide for him.

Even though it seemed like an eternity, it really wasn't. 'Eleu's head was down as if in prayer, but he could not form words. He just saw little grains of sand rolling around on the ground. Suddenly, he saw toes then ankles then kīhei. It was his love with her father at her side. She smiled and nodded. The answer had come, ua 'ae 'ia ke noi, the proposal was accepted. His loneliness vanished along with the little grains of sand.

'Ilima grew everywhere around the villagers' hale. Its low branching, woody stems had gray-green leaves and flowers spread all around. 'Eleu somehow got the idea of stringing those flowers to make a lei for his beloved when she arrived that day. How hard could it be? He saw women doing it, why couldn't he? After all, he'd fought and killed men in battle.

The yellow-gold double flowers were extremely delicate and took hours to string. He was lima nui, big thumbs, and seemed to crush nearly every flower he touched. Finally in desperation, he asked for directions from a neighbor woman who only laughed at his crooked two-inch lei.

"It takes five hundred flowers, 'Eleu. At this rate, it would take you a month, and they would be dead by then." She snatched it away from him. He was wounded to the core.

Kahikina came with her family. 'Eleu managed to put the 'ilima lei over her head not exactly proud of his failed experience; however, he had gathered maile to place on the shoulders of her and her family. They were obviously pleased.

In the interval between his asking for her hand and that day, he managed with help of neighbors and use of borrowed tools to construct hale of pili grass. There was a hale moe for their sleep and a hale imu for their individual cooking ovens. For her, he built a hale ʻāina for her eating, a hale peʻa for her kapu time, and a hale kuku for her kapa preparation. His former hale mua would be his eating and worshiping place and for visiting kāne. The ʻohana looked on with pride and appreciation of his work. Well, at least he hadn't failed in that respect. They knew ʻEleu would pūlama his wife, treat her with loving care, and see that she was happy.

ʻEleu was so busy impressing his new love and her ʻohana, he had not realized that they had gifts for the new couple. She and the wāhine brought lauhala mats and fine kapa, some plain and others decorated with red, green, yellow and brown, all to grace their home. The family gave gourds, calabashes, food, and a koʻi kit with adzes of all sizes, ʻaha, hammerstones, rubbing stones, clamps, painting brush, chisels, caulking tool, and a pump drill, all wrapped in tough woven hau cordage and tied with ʻaha. ʻEleu was grateful for all the items but was staggered with the gift of the koʻi. His were quarried from Keanakākoʻi on top of Mauna Kea many years ago and had been given away when he had entered the lua school or lost traveling to many battles. The fine gift of tools were for many uses especially canoe making. He beamed. But the greatest of all the gifts that were produced that day was a wonderful fishing canoe and paddle. They were beautiful and of fine construction reminiscent of his own work. Running his hand along the grain lines, he stopped cold, feeling a familiar blemish in the wood. It was a long-buried bud of a memory.

Tears welled up in his eyes, but he managed to ask, "Where...did you get this?" Kahikina touched his arm in dismay.

The great-grandfather spoke for the first time that day, "There was a man who came here years ago. He was from Puna on the mokupuni of Hawaiʻi, a great warrior for

Kalaniʻōpuʻu. He said he had made it and left it behind, saying we might need it someday. Our family has used it ever since, and it never fails to come back full of fish."

ʻEleu fell silent. That was his father's own fishing canoe, the one he and his mother launched from Kī in Kapaʻahu. The story of how Kahikina's family acquired it was miraculous.

In the days to come, Kahikina was worried she was not pleasing her husband. She fretted over whether to say anything to him about his obvious sadness. One evening, she decided to broach the subject.

"My love, am I not pleasing to you in your life?"

He stirred from his reverie. "You are more pleasing to me…than all the ʻilima lei I could manage to make for you." They both laughed.

"I'm so sorry, my beautiful girl. I must tell you about the canoe."

ʻEleu related the story of the wonderful canoe made by his father, the death of his mother in childbirth, the loss of his father to despair, and the subsequent abandonment of his own little boy.

All came spilling out of him then finally "I am happy with you in my life."

The pair sat cross-legged in the waning light looking into each other's eyes. ʻEleu stroked his wife's beautiful hair then her cheek, and taking her chin in his hand, they touched noses.

"Let us go to our bed, my love."

Events in the lives of ʻEleu and Kahikina took shape over the next year. Kahikina became pregnant, and whatever she craved, her husband strove to give her. Young sweet potato leaves and hilu fish seemed to be the only things she wanted toward the end. The greens were good for her, and the desire for hilu foretold a quiet and industrious child.

When it was her time, the women of her family came from Kailua. Almost immediately, the first child came—a boy. Ānuenue they called him because his mouth was in a perfect little arch like a rainbow. All was calm for a time until she started to have birth pangs again. Her mother and aunt looked at each other in amazement. A head appeared with the umbilical cord twisted around the baby's neck. Kahikina's mother went to work to bring the child out of the birth canal. He was not breathing. She blew the hā into his little body, and he opened his eyes with the perfect little smile on his face. His name Kahāipo meant the sweetheart's breath as Kahikina's second son had none in him when he was born.

The two beautiful robust baby boys slept through the night and gave no trouble at all. 'Eleu cuddled his boys, watching their little mouths puckering into pouts or sucking on his finger or tiny baby fingers clutching his own. He was a happy man and loved those little boys, always dreaming of teaching them in the ways of the ancient ones.

After the Makahiki season in the early spring 1798, paddlers arrived at the beautiful white sand bay at Waimānalo. The villagers noted the landing, and word spread from hale to hale. All were on alert as the canoes were carrying royal kapa banners. They were seeking a man. One of the villagers led them to ʻEleu. He was working at weeding the ʻuala, an annoying ongoing struggle at the best of times but made easier by the soft oli sung by his wife to their little ones.

Shadows of the two men and their standards spread over the potato patch, and ʻEleu turned to look at them, shading his eyes.

"Are you the canoe maker's son?" one of them asked.

"I am." ʻEleu suddenly realized they were royal messengers and stood to bow.

"His royal highness King Kamehameha remembers you through Kekūhaupiʻo at Nuʻuanu and sends his greetings to you. He requests your presence and canoe-making skills at Pāwaʻa. He is building a fleet of large canoes and is in need of good men." They glanced at Kahikina and the two babies. She stopped singing in mid vowel, mouth open.

ʻEleu swallowed hard, his mind racing. The word no was not an option. They watched him with little emotion, waiting. After a few seconds he heard himself say in a dead voice, "I will come."

Again, the men looked at Kahikina. "We will stay the night and take you with us tomorrow." The two men turned on their heels and left unceremoniously. The villagers would look after them. ʻEleu thought of the messengers' kindness.

His heart sank. He knew what that meant, probably a long time away from his family. The men demanded he come immediately. He had no choice but to obey.

The only option available to him was to contact Kahikina's family. He sent a young neighbor boy to run to Kailua to beg for someone to come. Her brother ʻOluʻolu arrived that afternoon. He assured ʻEleu he would stay and help especially the great-grandfather who was very ill.

Early next morning, the men came for ʻEleu. The parting was horrible. He tried to memorize his wife's face and the faces of his infant sons who were crying. He was torn between his family and his allegiance to the king. The men turned their backs to attend to the gear ʻEleu had assembled including his koʻi, and left for the beach.

"I don't know how long this will be. You know it is not far…just over the Koʻolau at Waikīkī Ahupuaʻa," he said. He and Kahikina clung to each other for a long while. The men waited in the canoes.

"Why is there always this terrible tearing away?" ʻEleu groaned in her ear.

She whispered, "It won't be long, my love." ʻEleu was not so sure.

The little family stood on the beach, waving as the canoe pushed off. ʻEleu's heart was somewhat relieved that her brother was by Kahikina's side. He raised his hand as if touching their hands across the empty space and watched his family disappear as the canoe made its way southeast around Makapuʻu.

Pāwaʻa was a busy lagoon where war canoes were in various stages of assembly. ʻEleu was housed with many men from Oʻahu, Niʻihau, and Kauaʻi in a large hālau thrown together for the king's work. Many hālau waʻa had been erected to protect the work from the sun.

ʻEleu was given the job of finely tuning the hewed koa logs brought from the upper regions of the west end of the Waiʻanae range. The trees were not as big as those found at Hilo and near Kealakekua on Hawaiʻi Island, but they were as strong and would make worthy war canoes. Other woods were being used as well: wiliwili and hau for ʻiako (outrigger boom), hau for ama (outrigger float), ʻōhiʻa lehua for masts, and ulu for moʻo (gunnels). Paddles were usually made of koa or koaiʻa.

'Eleu wondered how many canoes were needed. He suspected they were probably for an invasion of Kauaʻi, the last island that had not been conquered by Kamehameha. He went on with his work, hours turning to days and weeks turning into months. He managed to snag runners sent with messages for more wood products to get word to his family. Usually, a message came back by way of the runner. The family was fine and awaiting his swift return. The twins were growing.

As 'Eleu steadily did his work, he became friendly with some of the men. One man in particular caught his attention. They would eat together and discuss the days' events and various aspects of canoe production. The man called Waipā was from Kauaʻi and a highly skilled canoe maker. He liked to discuss possible ways of building canoes especially out of wiliwili wood. 'Eleu was a bit skeptical, and they debated the folly of using such a light wood. Their discussions turned to the building of the great ships coming into Kākuhihewa, Honolulu Harbor, which Waipā had been studying. With all the iron that was circulating in the islands, blacksmithing had been learned by many kānaka. Waipā was an expert, turning bits and pieces of the iron he could acquire into nails.

Other days, their conversations would turn to the conquests of the great king. Waipā was impressed by the king's kindness and generosity toward the makaʻainana after the horrific battle at Nuʻuanu. Waipā was also impressed by 'Eleu's stories of the battle.

"I've heard the man actually dug and planted with his own two hands," Waipā marveled.

"It is true," 'Eleu related. "You see what he did here, and I've seen Kūāhewa, the huge cultivated area our aliʻi created in the uplands above Kailua, Kahaluʻu, and Keauhou on the kona side of Hawai'i. Chiefs and commoners alike worked together with their o'o (digging sticks)."

One early morning, royal messengers came to Pāwa'a to request some men especially 'Eleu and Waipā, who would be going to the navy yard at Kealakekua. 'Eleu recognized two of those men who came for him at Waimānalo. He agonized over the turn of events. There was no time to get word to his family. Somehow, he must let them know where he was going.

Work at the bay on Hawai'i Island was the same. Hundreds of logs had their cores removed and the pepeiao gouged out inside at intervals. Seats fitted with the wae underneath would prevent the hull from twisting. Those seats would hold two paddlers each. With the addition of the platform between the hulls, the combined carrying capacity of the peleleu could easily be two hundred forty paddler-warriors plus gear. The sails made of canvas were attached to 'ōhi'a lehua masts, resembling the schooners that came to the islands. The new sailing vessels were called wa'a peleleu, the large war canoes for Kamehameha's approaching invasion.

'Eleu was good at all the canoes' lashing with 'aha. Beside his duties of finishing hulls, he was requested to tie the intricate pā'ū o Lu'ukia, the decorative and strong lashing by which the 'iako (outrigger boom) was attached to the canoe.

During the day, 'Eleu worked hard to keep himself from thinking. The nights were not so lucky. He rolled around on his pallet dreaming, constantly dreaming of his family. Maka pilau, evil ghosts, robbed him of his sleep. He usually awoke in drenching sweats and foul moods. 'Eleu's only comfort was his friend Waipā.

Then it happened. A ship appeared in the bay at noon. Sailors came to trade iron for food and water. The canoe makers stopped to observe the movements of the boats lowered off the ship with barrels in tow, sailors swarming over the boarding nets spread out over the sides. 'Eleu never looked their way and began gathering his tools. It was time for the noonday meal. He was hungry and in another foul mood. He did not care anymore about the big ships.

The sailors came and went from the shore to the ship at Ka'awaloa and Ke'ei. Back and forth, they came until it was too dark to see. The women from shore tried to come aboard under the cover of night, but the captain would not allow it and sent them packing. He had another thing in mind.

Early the next morning, some sailors were hiding on shore by Ka'awaloa Point for "that other thing." 'Eleu had gone alone for a swim in the half-light of the bay to wash off the stench of the night's sleepless trauma and was surprised that the ship was still anchored in the bay. He finally felt refreshed and went back to shore and picked up his kit to begin the day's work. All the while, his only thoughts were of his family. His inattention to his surroundings was something a warrior would never do. The men quietly followed their excellent candidate who was easy pickings. 'Eleu felt a stunning blow to the back of his head. All was blackness, and he again was fighting the maka pilau.

PACIFIC NORTHWEST COAST (1799)

'Eleu heard the oars' rattle in the oarlocks of the rocking boat and the lapping of waves against the side of a ship! He suddenly remembered something odd for no reason at all. It was his birthday, February 1799. He had been gone from his family for nearly a year! The boat knocked against the ship several times as it rolled in the ocean's swells, and when he finally opened his eyes, some sailors were hooking ropes to iron rings on the sides at the bow and stern to be hoisted aboard. 'Eleu was in the bottom of the boat. A sailor sneered at him. Nausea overcame him as he stared at the ugly man, smelled the unwashed sailors and the foul odor of the rotten garbage at the bottom of the boat, and felt his head spinning as he tried to stand. 'Eleu saw another boat following close behind, and there were two canoes trying to catch up for last-minute trade or so he thought. He tried to call the paddlers for help, but the sailors manhandled him. 'Eleu managed to deck a few of them with an unwelcome bath in the sea. There were too many though, and one of them drove his fist into 'Eleu's midsection and pushed him up the steps protruding on the ship's side. Trying to catch his breath and hanging on to the rope hand railings to keep from falling backward, 'Eleu tripped and sprawled on the ship's deck. He thought to himself, "So this is the realization of my dream of sailing on the big ships?" He did not know the word yet, but he had been shanghaied!

The man behind kicked 'Eleu. "Get out of the way," the white man shouted at him and threw his adze kit to the deck with a clatter. 'Eleu was grateful to see them. Then the man picked up two large bags of kalo, threw them over his shoulders, and disappeared below deck.

'Eleu was beginning to come out of his stupor. There were ropes of all sizes, some as round as a man's arm, wound around pegs, and draped and dangling from places he could only guess. Big white kapa, which he then recognized as canvas, was rolled around branches of the tall leafless trees, the masts, and he only glanced at the wood planks daubed with caulk beneath his feet. Iron nails, which the natives looked on with an eye to covet were everywhere. With his head swimming, he could hardly take in the bulk of it all.

'Eleu suddenly noticed a commotion between those two canoes and the boat a short distance from the ship. Some of the sailors were struggling with two of the paddlers. One of the paddlers was Waipā who had witnessed the abduction. Just before the canoe was capsized by the sailors, he managed to shout "I'll tell your 'ohana!" 'Eleu raised a grateful hand in recognition before he was shoved away from the ship's railing. Waipā and the other paddler righted their canoe, and the two made their way back to shore.

Some sailors began stowing the few provisions being brought aboard. A barefooted sailor in a faded striped shirt and three-quarter length frayed pants, which seemed to be the uniform of the men on board, was at 'Eleu's elbow with a large bag of potatoes. The man nodded at the stores waiting to be carried below. 'Eleu grabbed his adze kit and a bag of coconuts to carry down into the na'au (the guts) of the ship. He tripped and slid but managed to catch himself before he hit bottom. So far, he was not doing very well.

Last minute items were quickly stored below, and the water barrels were lashed on deck with ropes while some casks were lowered below decks. Buckets hanging on hooks on the walls needed to be filled. The sailor pointed to the buckets. 'Eleu nodded he understood. Then the man showed him the canvas hammock he would use. 'Eleu had a question on his face.

The sailor said in disgust, "Like this." And he jumped into the hammock. He then pointed to a seaman's chest where the Sandwich Islander could stow his belongings. 'Eleu was only wearing a malo when taken, so the sailor brought him some clothes since he had no money to buy them in the ship's store.

When the man left, 'Eleu was all alone and managed to sit in his hammock. Bewildering tears welled up in his eyes, streamed down his face, and fell on his bare chest. "No!" he thought, "This will not be. I will figure this out. I will toughen myself again as a koa." Suddenly, he felt 'ōkala, his skin crawl. It was his own great-grandfather Ka'ōka'i, turning his head again to the future. "Eō, e kuʻu kupuna kuakahi ē! Yes, great-grandfather, I am still listening!"

On deck, the bosun's pipe sounded and all hands assembled. 'Eleu heard a voice giving orders, mostly unintelligible to him although he managed to understand a few words. Over the course of his years, he had encountered more and more white men's English, which was becoming familiar. However, there was still a lot to learn as he moved into this new adventure thrust upon him.

Suddenly, a short red-faced portly man appeared from below. He wore a green waistcoat stripped of all its buttons except for two which seemed ready to fly at any moment. There was a bit of white fluff at his neck. Over the vest was a knee-length brown coat which flared out behind as he walked. The coat had a stand-up collar and triangular lapels that rested on his rotund chest, again with missing buttons. His trousers were tied just below the knee, and he wore boots instead of hose and shoes as was the fashion of the ship's officers.

"Are those barrels secure, Mr. MacKenzie?" the man shouted in a blustering voice over the din of pig squeals and chicken cackle, another button popping off. James Cavanaugh, was the supercargo in charge of the trade goods and its sale and represented the owners on board the ship. The button kept rolling back and forth over the deck before it clinked down in a deck grating.

"Aye, sir." The first mate, Mr. MacKenzie, suppressed a snicker.

'Eleu's eyes darted here and there, watching the sailors gathered around. His heart leaped for joy noting the presence of kānaka on board, one younger than 'Eleu and two older. They would become his mentors in learning the ropes and explaining in 'ōlelo maoli, his native tongue. Two of them worked above in the sails. The third was a cabin boy to the master. 'Eleu just stood there not knowing what to do. The cabin boy grabbed 'Eleu's arm and moved him to a spot where he would not be in the way.

The master of the ship Mr. Micah Stevens, who was tall and handsome with a shock of coal black hair and dressed exactly opposite of the supercargo, came from below decks, clapped his tricorne hat on his head, and began giving orders.

"Mr. MacKenzie, the wind is picking up. All hands to their stations. Away aloft. Secure the guns, Mr. Neilsen." The pipes sounded again, and there was a general scrambling everywhere.

"Stand by there at the capstan...Anchor up..."

The men put the levers into the holes of the capstan and began pushing those long poles round and round. 'Eleu watched the rope filling the vacant area of the capstan and wondered about its whereabouts. The anchor was secured to the side of the ship.

The two Sandwich Islanders went aloft with the sailors. 'Eleu watched as they swiftly took to the upper regions, climbing up the shrouds. They were on the spars in no time, letting loose the sails which dropped down. Men below were pulling on ropes threaded through pulleys and tying the sails into position; they lowered themselves to the deck below by ropes or the shrouds.

"Guns secure, Mr. Neilsen?" 'Eleu was astonished when he heard the master say that. Of course, there were cannons on board. Even a merchant ship needed protection with four six-pounders and two nine-pounders, fore and aft. Canon balls lined the grating on the deck.

"Aye, sir." Mr. Neilsen, a tall Norwegian, was the gunner and in charge of all weaponry.

"Everything secure aloft, Mr. MacKenzie?"

"Aye, sir."

With the anchor up, the ship's head was brought around. The sails caught the wind and 'Eleu drew in his breath. He could feel the ship as a living thing, moving forward on the sea beneath it. It was full and heavy, and it rocked.

Seizing him was a longing for his wife's loving arms. He watched the sails above his head become full, slapping as they did with the wind. She made her way out of Kealakekua Bay and rounded Ka'awaloa Point.

"Starboard to helm, let the wind take her."

The helmsman obeyed with "Aye, sir."

The ship was a two-masted merchant brig out of Boston which was owned by a group of men wanting to make good money in the trading business. It was called the *Marguerite Anne*, named after the owner's wife. There were many ships on the seas bringing with them items from America's East Coast for the coveted otter-skin trade with the Indians on the Pacific Northwest Coast. After a brief stint in the Sandwich Islands to rest and trade for provisions, in many cases the next leg of the voyage was to Canton, China for more trade then back to the Northwest Coast. However, the ship would only remain long enough in the islands to re-provision then would go directly to the Coast. Unbeknownst to 'Eleu, it was also a smuggling ship.

They crossed the rough 'Alenuihāhā Channel at the northern tip of Hawai'i Island and skirted the southern coast of Maui past Lahaina. 'Eleu hoped against hope that the ship would stop at Kākuhihewa that he might jump ship.

After picking one port clean of necessities, the traders' habits were to move to the next port, ensuring the crew's survival for voyages of many months. Travel to the Pacific Northwest Coast took only about a month. The water supply on board would be sure to fill their needs for drinking, cooking, and washing. Fresh produce and live pigs and fowl would be available right away while root vegetables and salted pork were for future use. The ship also took shanghaied men, ensuring the crew was a full one.

"'O wai kou inoa (What is your name)?" asked the kupuna of the three kānaka as O'ahu came into view. He looked to be around fifty years old.

"'O 'Eleu ko'u inoa (My name is 'Eleu)."

In the traditional greeting of honi, they touched the sides of their noses to the snickers of the sailors around them doing their chores. The four kānaka stood together at the railing as the ship skirted past Kākuhihewa, tears flowing down the old man's face. 'Eleu could guess at the reason. His own heart ached.

"What kind of name is that?" one of the sailors remarked interrupting the thoughts of the newest member of the ship's company and not used to the strange names of the natives. Repeating it, he pronounced it wrong. A couple others did the same.

"We'll call you Louie."

Another man walked by and said the same, "Aye, it'll be Louie, then." The name stuck.

The Sandwich Islanders went back to their work with their American names, the older men Jack and Billy, both topmen, and Tom the cabin boy.

The ship dropped anchor at Waimea on Kaua'i, and the Sandwich Islanders were herded below but not before 'Eleu attempted an escape to the railing and the sea below. He got the blunt end of a musket across his face, drawing blood for his effort. The muzzle ends were jammed into the chests of the men who were then locked in the storeroom. They were only let out when the trading ended and the ship was far out to sea.

"What course, sir?" the navigator asked of the master.

"Northeast to the coast and our destiny, Mr. Smith."

'Eleu was sick at heart, watching Kaua'i disappear as the ship steered toward whatever adventures lie in the mists and cold and forests of unfamiliar 'āina ahead. The ship was far to the east north east with the wind generally to the northwest of the islands and 'Eleu's family on O'ahu.

The weather was cool, pleasant, and generally cloudy with a great swell from the northwest. 'Eleu breathed deeply of the sea air devoid of the fragrances of his home, and again, his old friend *longing* accompanied him. He had spent much time on the sea in his canoes with paddles, but sails pushed the ship forward.

'Eleu was to be taught the ropes literally, and the names of the sails and all the other aspects of the ship. Jack and Billy would have to double their workload teaching 'Eleu, but they need not have worried as the canoe maker's son was a fast learner. In no time, he was up the shrouds and comfortable with working his way in the canvas along thick ropes. The first time, however, he had clung fearfully to the boom until prodded.

"Don't look down" was Jack's command. One could not have a fear of heights on that job. 'Eleu inwardly smiled at his new title of topman.

'Eleu memorized the parts of the ship, comparing them to canoe parts. The stern was the moamoa; the bow was the ihu wa'a; the hull was the kino; the waist was the kainaliu. Starboard was 'ākea, and port was ama.

The master and the first mate used the compass, chronometer, and sextant, all to steer their course. He thought of asking the master about those instruments, but postponed that idea as it was not appropriate. While on night watch, 'Eleu followed the stars like his ancestors before him and watched their positions change in the night sky. As they traveled northeast, 'Eleu kept his eye on Hōkūpa'a, the kanaka name of Polaris, the North Star and the name of his mother's sister.

'Eleu had become adept at the use of the hammock. The first few times, he had flipped right over getting in or managed to wind up on the floor when he turned in his sleep. But that was behind him as were many things. One evening when the kānaka went for their dinner, they spoke in hushed tones in their own language. Jack related the story of his life in the canvas. He had been shanghaied as well but from Oʻahu. Mākaha was his home. Telling the story brought tears to his eyes. He had a wife and three children and had not seen them for five years. He like 'Eleu had dreamed of going to foreign lands, but he had not expected such harsh treatment. He was a captive.

Billy and Tom were actually brothers from Niʻihau who had been on another ship that went to China. The ship had been seized by pirates, but the two boys managed to get on another ship that was heading to the coast and then to Boston. Their adventures had been exciting. Unfortunately, they were hired on board the *Marguerite Anne* in America, and so like Jack, they just wanted to go home. The word shanghaied to fill out the ship's complement was explained to ʻEleu—it was a new word. In ʻōlelo maoli, kanahai. One of the seaman had died under mysterious circumstances. ʻEleu was hired on in stealth to take his place.

"And don't be nosy, ah…nīele about the dead man," Jack whispered in a mix of English and Hawaiian.

ʻEleu lay in the dead man's hammock, swaying in the dark and listening to the creaking of the heavy timbers above his head and the sounds of the sailors in their sleep. He wondered how he had managed to wind up in the bowels of a ship and thought about the happenings in his life that got him there.

He recalled the time when he was five years old in front of his family's hale moe long years ago. Many questions came to his small mind back then, and as a grownup, doubts had no answers. But ʻEleu smiled to himself, remembering that happy time when his mother Kamahinaohōkū, full moon of the night, could comfort him with a caress. No more would the maka pilau disturb his sleep. He placed his family in the hands of his ʻaumākua and at the back of his mind. The bells calling for the next watch sounded as he finally fell into a deep undisturbed sleep after many, many months. Rays of a full moon washed over the ship.

Weeks passed, and daily life on the ship could be harsh with the cat-o'-nine-tails for even minor infractions. It was the bosun's mate, a Scott called MacCorkindale, who wielded that brutish instrument. He seemed to take a fiendish delight in his torture of the men and enjoyed jeering at the Sandwich Islanders. Master Stevens retired to his quarters when a beating began. 'Eleu shuddered at the sight of the scarred bare backs of sailors who broke the rules.

'Eleu kept the buckets full in the crew's quarters, scrubbed down the decks in slack times, and did his duty as topman up and down the shrouds as the wind called for it. He never got sick when the kai and makani, sea and wind, were rough and the small ship was tossed about. He tried not to evoke the wrath of any of the ship's company.

The wind was blowing a moderate breeze with pleasant weather one day when the master gave Mr. MacKenzie the order to have the cooper scald the water casks. There was great excitement among the officers and crew. 'Eleu smelled the land before he saw it, and there was floating debris with ducks, puffins, and cormorants flying around, but he had no idea what scald meant. Jack explained that they were nearing their destination and would need clean barrels to hold new water.

LAND HO!

"Land ho!" the seaman shouted from the crow's nest.

Master Stevens put the glass to his eye. All hands rushed to the railings as Norfolk Sound or Sheetkah as the Indians called it came into view, and 'Eleu got a knot in the pit of his stomach, a new land! He saw a snow-covered mountain in the distance. In fact, it was Mt. Edgecumbe, a volcano located at the American-pronounced Sitka.

'Eleu awoke early before the pipe would call all hands to their stations for anchorage in the Sound. Flinging water in his face and drying it on his sleeve, he threw on his coat worn to ward off the cold and pulled on his black leather square-toed shoes. They'd had a devil of a time trying to fit his big flat feet into a ready-made pair from the sailors' store. 'Eleu had never worn shoes, and most of the men didn't wear shoes aboard the ship except in the cold. The sailmaker, doubling as a cobbler, managed the job. On shore, 'Eleu's feet would freeze without stockings and shoes.

He quickly tied his hair in a neat braid at the back of his neck to make ready for the work to come, and he raced to the ship's railing. He wondered about what kind of men he would see and what manner of animals. The sailors talked about bear, moose, white or black-tailed deer, and birds with enormous wingspans.

'Eleu rushed to the galley to get his breakfast of poi, dried fish, eggs, and coconut. Thanks to the kindness of the cook, who kept the boiled corms for them, the kānaka managed to eke out enough makeshift poi from the last of the kalo.

With the bosun's pipe chirruping, the crew leaped into action, everyone scurrying here and there with their orders to make the ship ready.

The master called out, "Away the anchor."

'Eleu climbed the shrouds, tethering the sails to the spars and stole a glance at the foreign land. There was that mountain reminding him of home. "It surely looked like a volcano," he reflected.

On the first day, a cannon was discharged to alert the Indians that a ship had arrived. Their village was far from the anchorage. The long boats were lowered over the side and a shore party under the command of Mr. MacKenzie went for water as the sailors waited for the Indians. The Sandwich Islanders were allowed to go ashore with the party.

'Eleu was handed the white man's paddle. It did not look very efficient—long with a narrow blade. He stared at the backs of the coated sailors, waiting with the stick in his hand. Like a child, he watched and learned—oar in the oar-locks, both hands on the shaft, oar in the water, and pull! It worked, but he was disoriented. He could see the ship but not where he was going.

"Oars up," the steersman in the bow said as the boat sped to shore on a wave and scraped on the sandy beach.

The shore party started to the interior to find water and an easy track to roll the barrels once they were filled. A succession of trees and rain-rotted logs restricted their search; in places, cedar and spruce trees grew nearly to the edge of the water. The outer part of the Sound exposed to the sea looked promising, and a few of the men scouted for a mile and a half to where the sand changed to a rocky coast. However, spruce-covered cliffs and debris-covered shore blocked them, and the search was scrubbed by Mr. MacKenzie.

The second day began with a cry from the lookout in the crow's nest. "Deck, there! If you please, sir. Canoes coming off shore."

All eyes turned to see the Indian craft coming toward the ship. The pipes called all hands to the waist of the *Marguerite Anne*, and Mr. Cavanaugh began giving orders to the men for the trading, which would take place shortly. The boarding net was thrown over the side.

Shouts of greeting were heard as two canoes came close, the natives speaking in both English and their native language to the master. A sailor with a musket was placed in the crow's nest ever watchful for anyone pilfering anything that was not nailed down including the nails or actions construed as detrimental to anyone's life.

The natives were allowed on board, and the trade ritual began or so the master thought. Sea otter pelts could only be traded for muskets, red or blue cloth, molasses, and coats or knives. In Sitka, the Indians had the upper hand as they knew the high value of the skins from frequent visits by other ships. Strings of blue beads, mirrors, scissors, thimbles, and other trinkets much desired by the natives as presents, and to which they felt entitled, were given to coerce them. However, there were no skins to be had that day.

The last person to get out of one of the canoes was a very tall man who wore a heavy black fur coat and hat with flaps pulled down over his ears. Jack told 'Eleu that the man was from a place called Russia. He had seen some of those strange men the year before. A new Sandwich Island word was created for them, Lukia. There would be an outpost built and settled by those men. 'Eleu noted that the man was white and that he spoke in English to Master Stevens.

On the third day, the canoes came out again after setting up temporary shelters and making large fires on the shore. The real negotiations would commence after more presents were doled out. Buttons especially were highly-prized gifts to the Indians who usually sewed them all over their garments. 'Eleu could understand the white men's considerable use of buttons particularly in the cold. Buttoned up to the neck, a coat was more efficient, warmth in and cold out. Dire necessity made fumbling with buttons on the flap of his pants a nuisance. The Indians would argue that a white man's buttons on his coattails were unnecessary. 'Eleu could argue that buttons were not needed at all.

Finally, a price was set, one musket and a fathom or six feet of red or blue cloth per pelt. Other items were also traded, a seaman's coat or suit of clothes or a knife for a skin.

In the bay at Sitka, the waves lapped on the shoreline, and many Indian canoes lined the beach. When they went ashore to hunt, 'Eleu got a good look at the construction of those canoes, easily seventy to eighty feet long. He noted wood and decoration and the many different types of logs used. In his mind, he calculated the trunk would have to be as tall as the koa from his home island.

Some of the sailors disappeared into the dwellings of the natives while the hunting party got nothing for their trouble.

The end of the day was signaled by the bosun's pipe requiring lights out and silence from the crew, but 'Eleu could hear some of the crew talking quietly in the light of one remaining candle. He heard the word smuggling and decided it was best to pretend to sleep. Listening intently though, he heard that the *Marguerite Anne's* destination was Spanish California where foreign trade was prohibited. The smuggled items were manufactured goods of clothing, cottons, silks, lace, and alcohol brought by the ships from Boston in exchange for grain, beef, tallow, and hides. A huge profit could be made as those items were sorely needed in Sitka. The smuggling made it more lucrative for everyone along the Pacific Coast, but if a Spanish ship should capture them, there would be hell to pay—incarceration in a Spanish prison or worse execution. It sounded as if the ship was not going on to China with a stop in Hawai'i. His hopes were dashed. Sleep overtook his eavesdropping.

Bad weather was an issue on the Pacific Northwest Coast. March brought gale-force winds with icy sleet and rain lashing over the small ship, making it impossible for the crew to do any work. To stay out of harm's way along the rugged coast, they hunkered down in coves south of Sitka where there were small Indian encampments or villages to wait for the weather to clear. The Indians did not seem to mind a steady downpour however and came to trade anyway. Fog was a constant headache, and snow and sleet were an occasional problem when the deck became covered with ice. The next day could be the same or suddenly quite calm and almost pleasant. Then the boats would take advantage of the clear weather to go ashore to look for water and wood. The *Marguerite Anne* was on the coast for many weeks, trading off and on as weather permitted and skins were available.

On the morning of a water-seeking day, some of the crew saw deer tracks along the shore in the snow that had fallen overnight. Mr. MacKenzie chose a scouting party and motioned for 'Eleu to go along even though when handed a musket, he pushed it away. He had seen them used at home.

Leaving the rest to fill the casks at a spring, the men started off through the dense forest. It was a laborious track at best, traversing snow-covered mountains of fallen trees or walking through ankle-deep boggy detritus. 'Eleu knew what made a successful hunt, quietly stalking the prey and using cover to hide oneself from the intended victim. The party suddenly came upon an open area, possibly a small green meadow in the summer but that moment, covered with snow, and there he was, a beautiful buck. He pawed at the snow, head bent down to get to the grass below. The hunting party froze in mid-stride. 'Eleu was afraid that the click of a gun would send the animal out of their reach. He was slightly in front and to the left of the group, and they saw the ever-so-slight signal of his right hand to stay back. For some reason, the men obeyed, and what they saw him do in an instant was beyond their understanding. With his left hand, he took that pīkoi, threw it, and dropped that buck like a rock. It never even had time to look up. The animal struggled mightily with his legs buckled under it, but the men were on it in an instant with that pīkoi still wrapped around the animal's front legs. Back on the ship, the men could not stop talking about the amazing feat they had seen as they enjoyed venison stew that evening. 'Eleu had proved his worth.

They finally had good enough weather to leave Sitka Bay area and begin their southerly route. The ship traded along the coast from many islands where there were good anchorages, cooperative weather, and Indians willing to trade.

'Eleu watched the land, sea, and weather and noted the nuances. When he was up the shrouds and into the sails at night or on night watch when the sky was clear, he noted the position of the stars as the ship moved from place to place. He also noted the different tribes' style of dress, modes of living, and of course, their conveyances. He was always observant of their actions and the manners of the crew toward them.

In areas where they found streams or falls to get water, 'Eleu would watch a sailor go about getting fish with a two-pronged spear. Despite his lack of success in throwing the spear in the lua school, his efficiency in using the new spear made him indispensable for getting all the salmon they could use. In the estuaries at the mouths of rivers, there was an abundance of shrimp, crabs, and lobsters, which could be had by using nets—another of 'Eleu's proficiencies. The sailors were becoming keenly aware of his cleverness and welcomed him along on their hunts.

Parry Passage was known for its difficult tidal currents. The Passage stood between Langara Island, where their destination of Cloak Bay was located, and Queen Charlotte Island. Master Stevens had heard sea otters were plentiful there, but the Indians were sometimes unwilling to bargain. He wanted to try his luck anyway. However, they were prevented from sailing through Parry Passage from the east by a violent gale. It did not seem likely they would make it into the bay. A great calm overnight caused them to quit the idea altogether because they could not get through the Passage without sufficient wind.

By dawn, 'Eleu noted the shifting flame of a candle stub and a sliver of sunlight dancing around the heavy beams of the crew's quarters. The pipes blew, and all hands were quickly on deck. 'Eleu was up the shrouds, Jack and Billy right on his heels. They stepped out along the ropes, bent over the spar, and untied the sail. The brisk westward wind was picking up, and the three kānaka shinned down the ropes while sailors below tied the loosely flying sails taut, and the ship was easily sent over the tidal currents.

They sailed into the bay and smoke was seen from several extinguished fires on the beach. Cloak Bay, between Cox Island and Point Iphigenia, was the most beautiful place 'Eleu had seen along the coasts. Weather-beaten trees lined the spectacular shore. Mists lay over the bay, rock pillars and a dramatic bluff were home to thousands of sea birds. The air was full of their cries. Jack knew their names—puffins, murres, and storm petrels. "Good eating," he'd said.

The natives from the village of Kiusta across the Passage had seen them coming. About ten o'clock, some canoes came off shore and a local chief named Keow came on board the *Marguerite Anne* along with some of his minor chiefs. Keow was dressed in the manner of an English gentleman, looking proud but rather strange with his long hair draped over his shoulders and a tricorne hat sitting precariously on top of his head. Master Stevens raised his eyebrows as the chief explained that he had been given a suit of clothes by Captain Douglas of the Ship Iphigenia ten years before. The Point was named for his ship. The out-of-date clothes were rather worn and moth eaten, but fit him well, and despite the incongruity, he looked remarkably good in them. 'Eleu noted Master Stevens took the chief to his cabin, clapping him on his shoulder and praising him for his good looks.

The other men wore furs and feathers and brought a mountain of otter skins on deck to be traded. Mr. MacKenzie and the other officers carried on brisk bargaining with them, exchanging many desired items for the expensive coveted pelts. It was a successful campaign with everyone satisfied.

Keow emerged from the master's quarters, his tricorne hat sitting cockeyed on his head, fully satiated with eat and drink, and acting rather tipsy. The arrogant master emerged smiling broadly that he had taken advantage of the chief. Just as Keow reached the ship's ladder, he stood proud and tall and smiled back at Stevens, knowing he had won. Jack whispered to 'Eleu that the cunning chief was actually quite brilliant, and the master was the stupid one, paying too much for the pelts.

They spent a week in the area trading with other villages on Langara Island and then down the eastern side of Queen Charlotte through Hecate Strait. They stopped at some places to trade and collect wood and water. Mostly, the shoreline was inhospitable, and sometimes, the natives were as well, refusing to sell to the white men at all.

When he was keeping busy, 'Eleu could usually hold his family at bay in the back of his mind, but for a few days, Kahikina and his boys weighed heavily on him. Loneliness, anger, and especially guilt over the enforced abandonment of them caught him up in a foul mood.

He was sent to shore on a wood and water-seeking day while the ship lay anchored in a small exposed cove. The weather became as foul as 'Eleu's mood. Mr. MacCorkindale, the bosun's mate, was in charge and hated all Indians including the Sandwich Islanders and decided it was time to get the big one. The question was how.

They were filling the casks at a spring, and suddenly, a small party of Haida Indians appeared. Mostly, they were curious, but the Haida had a reputation of not being the most friendly tribe, so the crew was apprehensive. MacCorkindale brandished a musket at them, motioning for them to go away. The group consisted of three warriors, a woman, and a child about nine years old. The warriors took what MacCorkindale thought was a provocative stance and stupidly fired, hitting one of their own and wounding the child who had moved across the line of fire toward her mother. 'Eleu immediately went to the child. Suddenly, everything went wild. The remaining warriors shot at them, and the shore party shot back.

"Get out of the way, you stupid kūkae!" MacCorkindale screamed at 'Eleu.

"You have insulted me, sir!" 'Eleu shot back at the Scot, wondering how he knew that word.

The mother swooped down and grabbed her child away. Everyone was reloading, and no one noticed the two warriors had disappeared as well as the woman. 'Eleu had never known the anger he felt at that moment and charged MacCorkindale full force, knocking him down then bodily picking him up and smashing him on his knee. Suddenly, all was quiet as the shore party realized that the bosun's mate was dead with a broken back.

"What have I done?" 'Eleu said to himself. His lua training had kicked in without thought.

The crew was stunned with the speed of what happened, and for a few minutes, no one spoke and no one moved. Questions hung in the air. How did he do that?

What to do? Take the body back to the ship? Bury it here? But what would they tell Master Stevens? Should they place 'Eleu under arrest?

Oddly enough, 'Eleu spoke first in his limited broken English as he pushed the dead man off him. "We will take him back to the ship, and I will give myself over to the master." Lowering his head, he picked up the man's body and carried it back to the long boat. The rest loaded the water casks.

"Lower a rope," 'Eleu demanded from a sailor above as they came close to the ship. He had a hard time making the man understand in the increasing noise from the storm.

Talk spread through the crew to the master, who appeared at the rail as the body was lifted aboard. The sea was really rough, banging the long boat against the side of the ship.

The master began giving orders. "Get those long boats and water casks aboard," he screamed at the men. "Get the ship out to sea. We're going to be smashed to bits on those rocks."

The weather took over any explanations. It was a huge gale, and the men including 'Eleu, who was forgotten about for the moment, were at the sails. The ship's crew was small, and the master could not afford to confine even one man. No one would sleep. In fact, no one would sleep for many nights as the sea continued to be heavy, and the winds raked the sails and broke the top mainmast.

The sea like 'Eleu's mind was the embodiment of the devil himself. For two days, they were pushed ahead many miles. Rain lashed the decks, washing some of the crew overboard, including the body of MacCorkindale and flooded into the lower realms of the ship. Mr. MacKenzie shouted at Master Stevens that the well in the bottom of the ship had six feet of water in it. The master ordered some men to the pump. Fright shown on his face, but 'Eleu was up the yards fighting with the sails and fighting the demon and did not care what was on the face of the master.

SHIPWRECK

The storm had propelled them over one hundred miles to the northwestern tip of Vancouver Island. It slammed the small ship broadside into the rocks at Cape Scot, causing a gaping hole in the larboard side. Water rushed in the breach. Master Stevens ordered the remaining crew to abandon ship, but strong gusts and shifting cargo caused the hull to keel over. The chaos on board was tremendous as the sailors scrambled to get their feet under them.

At first impact, 'Eleu had already descended to the starboard shroud. Thrown to the deck below, he landed on a large pile of coiled rope sliding on the wet deck to the larboard side of the ship. The angle of the capstan protected him from a falling spar, breaking barely a foot on top of him. Quickly, he pulled himself out from under the debris, a jagged deck plank ripping open his shoulder. The topmen including Jack and Billy were thrown from the sails and dashed on the rocks below. He watched them die in the heavy downpour. Other sailors had mortal wounds or were crushed to death under the weight of broken masts, falling spars, and loose cannon. Shrouds lay torn and strewed over the deck; planks looked like rows of shark teeth. Ropes and sails lay scattered over the hull or in the rough surf below.

'Eleu wondered at the fate of Tom, the cabin boy. Sailors who survived the initial impact tried to rescue some of their fallen comrades but were swept overboard by heavy swells and dashed on the sharp rocks. 'Eleu too was nearly flung overboard, but his fingers managed to grab a grating trapped on the broken deck boards that stopped his backward momentum. Any men below decks died under the weight of the collapsed starboard side. The heavy sea pounded the ship, splintering it to pieces. Everything was destroyed.

'Eleu heard death groans, screaming, crying, creaking, and all the hideous sounds of flesh, wood, and metal colliding with each other. The life was crushed out of each. The rain continued washing the blood from the wreckage and from his wound. He crawled to what was left of the railing and looked for a place where there weren't sharp rocks or debris and then dropped into the water below. There was no sound of anything living on board that ship. But again, he wondered about Tom.

Night was coming on fast, and 'Eleu needed to find a hole or cave into which he could crawl, away from the blasting wind and rain. There were many sea caves along the Northwest Coast. Maybe he could find one for himself. His long hair hung in strings over his body, and he could barely see with the rain stinging his eyes. His shoulder hurt, and with the adrenalin gone that had carried him through the last grueling days, exhaustion took its place. He staggered southeast about one half mile along a sandy shore. Visibility was poor, but there seemed to be a rocky shelf jetting out to sea that curbed the angry surf.

Finally, 'Eleu saw a depression in the cliff just above him, facing south and away from the wind. He climbed up to its mouth. There were some pieces of dry driftwood in the shallow cave, and he wished he'd had his drill from his adze kit. He, however, made do with pieces of wood for a makeshift drill and base and a bit of kindling to ignite a small flame as he had done many times at home. It seemed to be an abandoned bird's nest. "That was lucky," he thought or not so as he contemplated the existence of those items in a depression in a cliff. Had it been the home of some big bird that the sailors talked about? If one came back to reconnect with its failed nest, he would kill the thing and eat it for his supper. His mouth watered. The existence of driftwood in the cave was lost on him as he thought about the terrible hunger gnawing at him.

'Eleu could then tend to his wound, which was bleeding profusely. Fortunately, his sheathed knife was still on his belt, and he cut a bit of the bottom of his wet shirt for a bandage. That was that for the moment. Even with his painful shoulder, he fell off to sleep on the uncomfortable floor of the cave, grateful for the shelter and warmth. He didn't awaken until the next morning when light streamed into his den.

'Eleu winced from the pain in his shoulder when he tried to move. He stuck his head out of the cave and was happy to see a clear cloudless morning with light breezes. The top of the cliff was only about ten feet away. Carefully, he moved out of the shelter, dexterously climbing the face. When he arrived at the top, there was a grassy bluff and a forest just beyond, but then he turned to face the sea. What he saw caused him to retch. The horrible hulk of the ship, jagged against the blue sky, had seemed invincible on the open ocean. It was unrecognizable at that moment, like a toy boat smashed by an unhappy child. Up and down the shrouds, pulling ropes, stretching canvas, talking, eating, laughing— "all those men and my brothers are gone," he thought painfully. 'Eleu dropped to the grass and cried bitter tears from the horrors of the last few days.

When he could cry no more, he sat up and looked around. Where was he? The next leg of the voyage of the *Marguerite Anne* before it was hit by the storm was Vancouver Island. He remembered the stories of George Vancouver and King Kamehameha meeting in Hawai'i. Was he then on Vancouver Island? What would he do? Where would he go? His thoughts of going home on the *Marguerite Anne* were dashed on the rocks along with the ship.

He must salvage what he could. Walking along the cliff's edge, he found a crevice where he could easily climb down to the rocks below. 'Eleu found a water barrel that was not smashed to bits and still had its lid intact. Best of all, it was half-full. Tasting it, he found the water sweet not brackish. Drinking his fill, he checked for leaks in the barrel and found none.

The wreckage of the ship was mountainous; everything was jumbled together, and 'Eleu climbed around it with considerable difficulty. At the stern where the quarterdeck had been split open, he found some of the seamen's chests washed over by lapping waves. He hated invading the personal property of those men, but he desperately needed survival gear. He could not look at painted porcelain likenesses of wives and sweethearts or bits of ribbon-tied hair that were all ruined. "Coins might be a necessity later," he thought. Knives and other useful tools, he took with gratitude. He found soaked clothing and a bolt of cotton and a few yards of duck fabric, wet and covered with sand.

Miraculously while picking through the rubble, 'Eleu found his own chest, broken but still containing his adze kit and pīkoi in a canvas bag covering the tough woven hau. His shoes, coat, and extra set of clothes were covered with debris but usable. Finding a shovel and an ax was a stroke of luck. The question was how he would get the items back to his shelter. Everything was kept on shore. 'Eleu continued to scour the wreck, hoping perhaps to find food. Suddenly, a coconut floated by then a dozen more. He plucked them out of the water and added them to his supplies. His need to survive overrode the horror of dead bodies floating nearby or smashed on rocks and the fear of the returning tide.

Hours went by as he carefully worked his way to the bow, gathering bits and pieces where he could. He began accumulating great quantities of rope, rolling it up and cutting it where necessary—his mind untangling the possibilities as he untangled the rope. Over the noise of the sea and the creaking of the wrecked ship, 'Eleu thought he heard something but dismissed it. He heard it again and cursed the sounds that were confusing his senses. But yes, there it was a third time, coming from where the master's cabin should have been. A human voice was calling for help. It was Tom.

'Eleu began talking to the boy. "Where are you, Tom?"

He prayed, and his ancestors heard. The sea seemed to calm for just an instant.

"Here I am," the boy shouted as best he could. 'Eleu's ear went to the sound.

"I hear you, Tom. Hold on." 'Eleu began flinging rubble out of the way as fast as he could. A grating was the only thing preventing the boy's skull from being crushed. 'Eleu did not know what else might be crushed. Somehow, the boy managed not to drown in the motion of the waves. With debris removed, the boy's body was in full view, and there was blood washing around him—a lot of it.

"What hurts, Tom."

"My legs." The boy was crying.

'Eleu could not tell how bad they were. Cutting the hose and pants, he asked, "Can you move your legs."

"A little" came the faint reply, but only one leg moved.

Debris began floating around the boy, threatening to engulf him as the sea surged back through the ship. The wind was changing direction, and the sky started to cloud over. Whatever was going to be done would have to be done right that moment. Tom moaned as 'Eleu cautiously picked him up. Just then, the ship lurched toward the shore, and the pair simply stepped off.

'Eleu put him down. "Can you hold on to me around my neck?"

"I think so." 'Eleu shifted into position, and the boy grabbed hold. They would have to go back up the crevice then 'Eleu could come back for the salvage. It was a huge effort on both their parts, but they managed, and the boy was lain on the grass.

Back down on the shore, 'Eleu quickly wrapped everything in canvas then tied as much as he could into two bundles, using some partially intact shrouds. The sea grew violent and waves cascaded over the wreckage. Racing the ocean's waves, he hauled up one of the nets through the crevice then went back for the other. It was nearly impossible because of the heavy water barrel and a couple of times he lost footing and nearly fell; but with a mighty effort, all was at last on the bluff.

'Eleu was sitting for a moment trying to gather strength for what had to come next. He dared not carry the boy back to his shelter until he could assess the injuries. Using the water from the barrel to wash the boy's legs, he could see that one leg was crushed beyond repair and the other was badly lacerated. What could he do? He had no medication or clean cloths to wrap injuries, and the boy had lost too much blood. There was only one thing he could do.

He held the boy in his arms. Tom pointed to a coconut that had come loose from one of the bundles. With the butt of his knife 'Eleu cracked open the husk and poured a few drops into the boy's mouth. Tom smiled weakly, and his thirst was quenched with the reminder of home. He would not thirst or hunger again. Tom died in 'Eleu's arms.

Night was coming on. It was very cold. 'Eleu found the shovel in one of his large packs. Doggedly pounding the earth with that spade with sweat pouring from every part of his body, he cursed the powers that brought the two so far from their 'ohana and 'āina.

"This boy should be buried in the fashion of our ancestors, by his own family and in the embrace of his own land," 'Eleu shouted.

Shoveling dirt in the foreign method, he begged his mother Kamahinaohōkū, full moon of the night, to help him see in the darkness to bury this poor boy. With the grim job done, he thanked his beautiful mother for her tenderness in the light that accompanied his kuleana, that responsibility running through him and the blood of his ancestors. At least, the boy was buried decently. He could then go back and start another warming fire and sleep the sleep of forgetfulness.

But he was not to forget for in his sleep, he heard Tom say over and over, "E 'Eleu ē, mai poina 'oe ia'u!"

"No, Tom, I won't forget you." 'Eleu awoke abruptly to the sound of his own voice. "'O wai kou inoa Hawai'i? I don't know your Hawaiian name," he cried out in anguish.

Suddenly, he was drawn to the smell of smoke. He peered over his shoulder, and the light of day revealed an odd thing. There was his water barrel floating outside. He had lowered it the night before to the sand as there was no room for it in the cramped quarters of the cave. He sat bolt upright and discovered he was sitting in a puddle of water and realized the reason why the bird abandoned its nest. Coughing, he quickly retrieved and secured his barrel. The ocean water had put out the remnants of the fire, and the resulting smoke filled his cave. He would have to act fast if he did not want to lose the rest of the rescued belongings. Tying the bundles together with the barrel, he threw the long length of coiled rope to the grassy bluff above. It held while he crawled out of the cave and scrambled to safety. The rising water helped to float the load, and he was able to retrieve all of it. Glancing toward the ship, which was mainly underwater, 'Eleu despaired of ever going back for salvage.

He shivered in the cold light of dawn and tried to remember where his coat was, but he had to get out of the nasty weather and not spend time looking for it. He headed for the forest beyond.

With Tom buried and the weather clear, he left his rescued belongings protected in the forest near some large rocks and decided to explore the perimeter of the north end of the island. Most of it seemed to be impenetrable with many tall trees of different types. Fallen decayed logs covered with slippery moss from the dripping branches above covered waterlogged and boggy detritus. He did not want to lose himself in the wilderness and decided to turn back and explore again the next day. Then suddenly, he caught a movement out of the corner of his eye. He stood stark still listening, there, another movement. It was something with fur or feathers, small or large, he could not tell. The only thing he moved was his eyes. The thing gave a low quack, and then another as if calling to a mate or juvenile. It didn't seem frightened though. The sound came from the right, and 'Eleu's eyes shifted. It was a kōloa, a duck, caught in some brambles of a delicious-looking blackberry bush. Quickly, he grabbed the bird and twisted the neck. It would make a good meal.

Going to where he left his gear, he found a clearing a little behind those rocks. It was protected by a very dense growth of trees like a high roof and partially surrounded by those large rocks. He managed to scrounge some fairly dry twigs to make a fire. The roasted meat satisfied his hunger, and the feathers and bones would be useful in the future. He had water and coconuts that could carry him for a while, but he needed to scour the area for more food and water for his survival. 'Eleu made a makeshift bed out of canvas sails and wrapped himself up in his coat. He curled up next to the warmth of the fire and was snug like his twin babies in his arms. "Oh, my 'aumākua!" He had not given any thought at all to his family since the horrible incident with the ship's bosun's mate! Exhausted, he cried himself to sleep, wrapped again in loneliness.

There had to be a way to survive in a completely unknown land with unknown obstacles. "Obstacles were a part of life," he reasoned. "Obstacles either crushed you or you went around them in some miraculous way or you untangled them head on."

SURVIVAL ALONG THE COAST

Each day, 'Eleu skirted the coast to check out the lay of the land. He found a sand neck separating Cape Scott from Vancouver Island, framed on both sides with crescent-shaped beaches. The sand neck would be covered by the high tide washing over it. Many bays lined the coast either rock strewn or with long stretches of sand where driftwood could be gathered. Some places were impassable on foot as spruce and red cedar trees came all the way down to the water's edge.

For food, he found birds and other prey and kept feathers and fur for trade and bones to make fishhooks. He experimented with twigs and branches suitable for bows and arrows and spears. In the evenings, he would untangle the largest ropes and make nets for throwing and catch nets for 'ōpae and pīhā (shrimp and small herring) and most important, an 'upena ku'u, a gill net for catching lobster. 'Opihi were for the taking and their fluted shells were useful for many things. Washed yardage of the cotton cloth would make malo for himself. Every day, he went farther afield, searching for food and items for use in surviving.

The canoe maker was always on the lookout for that just right tree which could be carved into his way off the island and out to a ship. He suspected, however, that no ship would risk coming close to the coast. He would have to move. Looking east, he saw land to explore across a large body of water. For the moment, he would stay close to Tom's grave.

Unfamiliar sounds came in the night, and there was no way to identify them. Always keeping the rocks to his back and his fire in front, 'Eleu felt he was protected fairly well from unknown wild animals. He hoped there was nothing larger or more threatening than that buck he brought down with his pīkoi, the same weapon used to trip up men in the lua school and that he brought down his own father with.

"Oh, my makua kāne," he said, startling himself with the sound of his own voice. "I have not thought about you for a long while." He closed his eyes and covered his face with his hands, shrinking from the scene of his father dying in his arms.

Keeping company with his own thoughts, he would go for days hearing only the waves or bird song or maybe seals jockeying for position on sunning rocks.

Roasting his dinner at night, he watched the firelight dance in the treetops and sorted through feelings about his father he long held inside. He was no longer angry with the man for his abandonment. It was just sad to think of all those years gone, lost for all time.

'Eleu turned his negative thoughts to something more constructive—the lei niho palaoa his father was wearing at the battle on O'ahu. That was the sign of an ali'i. Again, he asked himself why? But there was no answer, and he vowed to find one when he got home if he got home. He would go back to his old homestead, and maybe there, someone would know.

Shattering his thoughts was a hair-raising grunt. Something was rooting around behind his rock shelter. It sounded like a big pig. 'Eleu had a roasted duck leg half way to his mouth, dropped it, and reached for his spear. He knew what the animal wanted, and it was above him right that instant, ready to invite itself for dinner. As 'Eleu raised his eyes, he could feel its breath on him hot and heavy, and he sprang out of the way as fast as he could. The animal's huge frame smashed down to where 'Eleu had been sitting. He laughed to himself that his dinner was somewhere under that large lump of black fur. The bear charged him, and 'Eleu ran the spear right through the animal's heart. He had a nice fur coat for winter.

In the ensuing days, 'Eleu had the unsettling feeling of being watched. He had not seen any sign of human life where he was and had not ventured very far afield, but once in a while, there was a prickling on the back of his neck like someone was out there. Scouting a few miles south of the sand neck, he discovered a red cedar tree of approximately the right size for a single hull fifteen-foot fishing canoe. He made note of the tree and decided he would have to make a temporary camp near it to start felling and carving it out. Exploring the area further, he came upon a large saltwater marsh that seemed to turn back in a northerly direction. He scouted the sandy shore and then the mudflats. There they were, fresh footprints! He dropped into a low crouch and swept the area with his eyes. Nothing moved. After a few minutes, he backtracked the prints which led from a sheltered area in the forest on the marsh's south shore. A fire pit was still warm from the morning's repast. Again, he stopped, waiting and watching. Again, nothing moved.

'Eleu skirted the edge of the forest, making his way to the exposed rugged shoreline and thinking it better to retreat to his camp. Crossing at the water's edge, he entered the forest on the other side and turned to look back at the attractive marsh. It had ducks and other water fowl including something that was beautifully white and amazingly huge with a long neck. "Was this the big bird the sailors talked about?"

The feeling of being watched passed from his mind as he prepared the camp. Apparently, his stalker had disappeared as the fire became cold, and the footprints vanished with the tide. A shored-up sail would be his shelter. Unfortunately, the makeshift hālau wa'a made with logs and branches wasn't waterproof, but he made it a little better by putting his last piece of sail under the branches along with some of the tightly woven duck fabric so the canoe would be at least partially protected. There was a proper distance between trees for felling, and if he did it right, the closeness to the tidal marsh would help him float the finished canoe.

'Eleu found some suitably rounded driftwood along the shore, a pair matched enough for 'iako but only a straight piece for an ama. "Not buoyant enough," he thought. The choices would have to do for the booms and float. Since he was a perfectionist, he grumbled about not having wiliwili wood for a proper float. Suddenly, he found the humor in the situation and started laughing uncontrollably until his 'ōpū hurt and tears wet his face. There he was in an unknown wilderness doing the impossible by trying to survive, and he complained about such a small thing. He only hoped the wa'a would float.

Chanting his mo'okū'auhau at every phase of the work gave him his sense of place even if the 'āina was not right. It reminded him of his niche in the scheme of things, his life, his culture. And as he carved out the log, flying chips reminded him that he was a canoe maker's son. He worked from morning to night hewing out the log. Even without the 'elepaio bird, he had a sense that the trunk was good and would make a perfectly straight and worthy canoe. Red cedar would also do for his paddle.

Months went by and 'Eleu was nearly finished. When the tide began to come in, 'Eleu only had to pull the canoe with a rope to the edge of the marsh and wait for the water to float it. It was pure joy to see the canoe in the water, held together with remnants of rope he had salvaged from the *Marguerite Anne*. He thought about those strands of rope connecting all things. Pushing off over the water-covered mudflats, he paddled toward the ocean and found his creation superb. The trial run was a success.

'Eleu was free to be on the move, and he was anxious to do so. He blessed the surroundings that gave him protection, gathered up his belongings, and went to Tom's grave. He was in distress at the thought of leaving his brother behind buried in a strange land, but 'Eleu begged Tom's caring 'aumākua not to turn their faces against him and to show him the way into the spirit world of his ancient family.

'Eleu turned away, and the thought of his father crossed his mind. Nothing could be changed; he must move toward the future.

What 'Eleu had seen of the west coast of Vancouver Island was rugged. He had been in and out of many bays, coves, marshes, and river mouths, fishing and hunting in each. He was able to find good tasting limu, and the Tlingit at Sitka taught him how to find edible tubers, wild onions, and other tasty treats to go with his 'opihi. There were high mountains in the interior, and he noticed a dusting of snow on the heights. Summer had turned to fall, and he could feel the chill in the air, crisp and fragrant. It was new to him, and he liked the change. It made him wary though as certain berries and other edible plants began to die back; drying and smoking became important tasks.

'Eleu's new camp was in a cave at the back of a large sandy cove, well-hidden by trees. Smoke would be absorbed by the trees, thereby keeping his living accommodations fairly secret. A stream emptied into the cove and above it was a dammed lake alive with beaver and other fur-bearing animals. He caught prey and prepared skins for trade although he did not know with whom he would do the trading.

The ocean waters south and east of Vancouver Island were teeming with marine life. The constant flow of nutritious waters attracted resident killer whales, the orca in their black and white skins 'Eleu had seen at Queen Charlotte Island. There were all manners of living things beneath, on, and above the surface of the sea along with the great leviathans, migrating humpback and gray whales. As he fished from the ocean, he could see the bloom, the life-giving algae making a colorful scum on the surface; big and little predators were feasting in the delicious soup. His nets were full, and his hooks, dangling chunks of eel, worked their charm.

The wet fall season he experienced gave way to cold. He began to worry if he had enough food and wood to keep himself alive over the coming months. The rim of the cove where small waves lapped the shore was a froth of icy snow and sand. 'Eleu had fashioned winter clothing for himself as he'd seen the Indians wear at Sitka. Buckskin shirts and pants were sewn together with sinew using a bone needle as were knee-high moccasins with fringe and double-thick soles. His bearskin, tied about his shoulders, went down to his calves, and an ermine and rabbit fur hat kept his head warm. The remnants of rope he'd acquired from the *Marguerite Anne* were beginning to wear with use, and strands of elk tendons became his new rope of choice.

'Eleu discovered the underlying basalt rock of the island out of which he fashioned grinding stones, adzes, newa, pries with which to open shellfish, and a pounder to crush tubers. Shells were used for cleaning hides and cutting. He was beginning to understand the new place and how to make it work for him.

Bathing had been a difficult situation for 'Eleu from the time he was shanghaied in February. Four weeks aboard the ship without a daily swim in the ocean followed by a fresh or brackish dip was not to be had but only a quick splash of head and arms. On inland forays for water gathering, he managed a bath in a stream or a quick swim in the ocean. The sailors laughed at his cleanliness, which he passed off as not being enlightened in the preference for a clean body. Surviving on Vancouver Island, he was able to enjoy that daily ritual again, but with winter upon him, it was difficult because of the cold. He managed to fashion hide buckets for carrying water from the stream to his camp where at least, some of the chill was lessened by the warmth of the fire, and he was able to pour the water over himself. He did his best to wash from head to foot especially his hair and beard where 'ukus liked to take up residence. The lice could make things unbearable, and he was tempted to cut his beard, but 'Eleu chose instead to keep his face and neck warm.

After a few weeks of winter weather, he awoke one morning to an almost summer-like day, and by afternoon, the snow had melted completely. 'Eleu took advantage, threw off his skins and furs and ran bare-ass into the icy water of the cove. Once the initial shock wore off and his teeth stopped chattering, he began to enjoy his swim. He didn't get far, however, as he noticed a movement in the forest close to his camp. Calmly, he swam to the shore, going the last few yards underwater to clear his hair from his face as the man stepped out of the trees, and he stepped out of the water.

"Warrior," 'Eleu thought, "because those weapons are not just for hunting."

There was a hint of a smirk on the man's face as he surveyed the big man. 'Eleu didn't even think about his nakedness as his lua skills kicked in, his eyes ever watching for any hint of motion from this possible adversary. The Indian was standing between him and his weapons. "Never mind," he thought, "I don't need them."

115

The Indian brandished a spear in one hand and a dagger in the other. 'Eleu saw him tense up, and they began circling one another. Not one muscle on 'Eleu's naked body rippled, not one sinew strained. He showed the warrior a sluggish posture, acting like someone who had never fought before and thereby catching the man off guard. The Indian had a look of satisfaction on his red-painted face as if he knew he'd already won, but 'Eleu had the edge and charged the man, hitting him hard. The man's weapons went flying, and 'Eleu sat on top of him with both hands around the warrior's neck. The man was covered with oil of some sort, not much different than what 'Eleu was used to except for the stench. A slight squeeze caused his eyes to bulge. The man tried to wave him off, but 'Eleu had subdued the Indian's arms with his knees. Just before the Indian blacked out with death close at hand, 'Eleu relented. Jumping off the Indian, 'Eleu offered the recovering man a helping hand, but the warrior wasn't through with him yet and went after 'Eleu's face with his fist. That was a mistake! Before the man knew it 'Eleu had him turned around with a choke hold and his fist in the middle of the warrior's back. Again, 'Eleu relented, not wanting to kill the man. The man went limp, giving the new opponent the silent nod of approval. They were enemies no longer. The warrior quickly gathered his weapons in defeat and disappeared into the woods.

In the cave's interior, 'Eleu slumped to his sleeping pad and panted like a dog with sweat pouring down his body and that oil stink about him. He had not fought in a while and was completely exhausted. Cooling down, he went to the stream and washed the salty oiliness from his skin and finally felt refreshed, but from that moment on, he would be on guard at all times. He would not be caught with his pants down ever again! He smiled.

The evening turned cold with the sunset. He stood at the mouth of the cave and watched the glorious beauty of the country surrounding him. The green flash appeared as the golden sun disappeared below the line splitting sea and sky, and the glassy water reflected the diminishing light. It was then the blue time, the twilight that precedes the black of night. He let it envelop him, but it did not last for long as the fire's light in the cave behind him caused his figure to grow long over the darkened shoreline. 'Eleu wished it would go all the way across the ocean to his home and wrap his family with love. He withdrew into his home in the cave, excruciatingly alone.

'Eleu relaxed though ever watchful and debated if he should move his camp. The warrior's tribe undoubtedly knew where he was by that time. The man had excellent fighting techniques but was obviously surprised by the foreigner's ability. 'Eleu would wait, sharpen his skills, and see what would happen next, and happen it did.

A hunting party of many canoes piled high with sea otter carcasses showed up on his front door step. The cove's shore was covered with them. Many of the natives were walking in circles around 'Eleu's own canoe. "Were they admiring it or desiring it?" It had been the men's voices that woke him. He jumped up and presented them with an appearance that caused exclamations and pointing fingers. Only in his malo and trying desperately to grab his bearskin, the Indians looked on in amazement at the large man. 'Eleu stood head and shoulders above them gazing over the crowd before him. They touched his dark skin just like theirs, admiring his tattoos. While looking at his wrapped malo, and studying the cotton fabric with which they were familiar, they saw his dwelling, obviously appreciating the choice location. When they began prying into his belongings, 'Eleu wasn't happy, but there were too many of them for him to protest.

They chatted among themselves until 'Eleu, hearing a couple of English words asked, "Where is the king among you?"

A few faces showed recognition of his question, and a man came forward bearing on his person a beautifully woven, striped blanket in white, gray, and tan. 'Eleu had seen those blankets along the coast as the *Marguerite Anne* traded with the natives. Mountain goat wool was used to make the thick warm garment. Sometimes, it was just thrown over the shoulders. Sometimes, there were two sewn together, making sleeves on the sides and worn down to their calves. Most of them had deep fringe.

The king took off his blanket and threw it around 'Eleu's shoulders. It was a great honor. 'Eleu in turn disappeared into his shelter emerging with an armload of fabric, and the man's pleasure showed on his strikingly noble face.

The warrior 'Eleu had fought stepped up next to the king. He was obviously second in command as the others deferred to him, and falteringly said, "Kala mai. I sorry no talk before fight. King not pleased with me but much pleased with your gift."

"And I am with his." 'Eleu stroked the beautiful wool. "You speak my language?"

"A little. You people visit frequently on board white men's ships. None of my people like your tongue as it is hard to pronounce. I have no problem. You stay in my house."

Wary, he accepted their invitation, considering the company of other human beings more desirable than his present situation. Maybe too, it was not wise to upset a potentially explosive situation. He could not tell whether they were nosy or helpful as all his items were packed into the canoes. Baskets of dried smoked fish were brought out as well. The king and warrior nodded their approval and then turned their attention to his canoe and broader paddle, getting in the craft to see how it moved on the water with those strange extensions.

'Eleu stepped into his creation, accepting his passengers and beginning a new chapter of his life.

The contingent of Indians paddled south with their newly-acquired friend. 'Eleu had a close-up view of the efficiency and beauty of their canoes, long but wide, a higher manu, and highly decorated. They could carry a big load. The warrior sat behind him, giving him a running commentary about the hunt, the felling, the carving, and something about hot rocks and water that had to do with their dug-out canoes. The man's jumbled English, Hawaiian, and his native tongue was difficult to understand, but he kept talking anyway. After some time, the entire entourage turned east into a large body of water.

The man was chattering on about Captain Cook and Bligh Island. 'Eleu was stunned by the name Bligh. "Was that the same man who had rescued me, Ka'ōka'i, and Wai'aha from our sinking canoe at Kawaihae so long ago?" The king grunted something in English about the canoe's dexterity and craftsmanship by the foreigner. 'Eleu smiled to himself, paddling with pride.

The waterway turned north, passing some small islands and a deserted village in a cove on the shore. In the warrior's continuing narrative, the English words Friendly Cove slid easily off his tongue. 'Eleu heard the sailors talking about the exact location where the Indians were great traders. That apparently was Nootka Sound which would have been the next stop for the *Marguerite Anne* had she and her men survived. So far, 'Eleu was in the right place.

LIVING WITH THE NATIVES

It was a long distance to paddle before they came in sight of cedar plank houses crowded together along the shore at the end of a cove. Even more incredible were the carved poles in front or alongside the houses or projecting out horizontally from the ridgepole. 'Eleu judged them at maybe three feet in diameter and as tall as a good-sized canoe standing on end. Carved and painted in fanciful designs of eagles, bears or other animals, they were totems and made an impressive sight.

'Eleu would live in the house of the defeated warrior. He worried it would be awkward but subsequently found the man to be most hospitable and a person who seemingly admired his conqueror. At least, he spoke English and some Hawaiian. The king only spoke a little English. 'Eleu's English was pilau—it stunk.

Upon entering the house, 'Eleu was stunned by the enormous building. As usual, his practical mind ran over the dimensions, thirty feet wide by at least one hundred feet long. The ridgepole and the supporting structure were made of massive cedar logs, and the planks of the roof and walls were three to four inches thick, overlapping each other horizontally. There was only one small door at either end of the house.

Right in the center was a mammoth fire pit hung with a copper pot of boiling liquid. Smoke and steam were drawn out of an opening in the roof. Another curious thing he noticed was what looked like boxes with something cooking inside. Every now and then women would throw hot rocks from the fire into the stewed mix boiling hard in the boxes.

"Copper pots? Where would they get those? From trade? And the boxes…?" 'Eleu pointed to them as the warrior led him to another box with a lid against the wall where all his gear would be stored. The dirt beside it was for sleeping. The thick wool blanket he was given by the chief was removed from him and placed on the ground. That instant of course, he was nearly naked except for his malo. It didn't seem to matter as most of the men were completely naked in the fire-heated house.

"We trade with north tribe at potlatch. They make copper. Planks are bent with steam."

The name of that tribe Kwakwaka'wakw[5] tripped easily off his tongue but not so into 'Eleu's ears, so many tongue clicks and guttural sounds. The concept of bending wood in that manner was also foreign to him. Maybe someday he might meet the copper-trading people and learn about their interesting ways. He was trying to digest what potlatch meant but was interrupted in his thought as the man invited him to eat and pointed to another decorated box to sit on. The Indians were sitting on many boxes with their legs curled up under them. Evidently, those boxes were their furniture and were also used for storage of skins, cedar bark clothing, tools, and trays of food.

"Do these people all live here?" 'Eleu's face showed his concern.

The man waved off his question. "This winter camp" which would explain why the houses were so close together on the shore of Tashees; it was a smaller cove and colder. The abandoned camp he saw at the opening of Nootka Sound was their summer camp.

It was rather cramped sharing quarters with twenty five other people and reminded 'Eleu of the hale mua, the men's eating house, where sometimes a dozen or so would be welcome. Their hale moe, or family sleeping house, only held

---

5.   Meaning: Kwak'wala-speaking-people. (Kwakiutl in English)
      Port Rupert, Vancouver Island, BC

the immediate family. But for kānaka, the two were never combined. He started to worry. "What if the women of this apparent extended family sleep here too?" His question went unasked and was interrupted by a woman handing him a tray containing fish, boiled to a broth-like state and to be eaten with a clam shell, and spawn with whale oil poured over to be eaten with fingers. It was rather tasteless especially with no salt, and the oil was nasty tasting. 'Eleu was too hungry to be picky.

The warrior pointed to the woman and said, "Kauwā."

"Kauwā?" He wasn't talking about the food; that word meant servant or slave in 'ōlelo maoli. 'Eleu shuddered, thinking of those people kept at home in Nīnole, Ka'ū district, for sacrificing at the altars of the luakini heiau in ancient times. What he saw was a pretty round face with a pleasing figure and discovered while looking around, she was not like the rest of them. Nothing was mentioned of her tribe. He hoped death was not her end in the place.

Again, he was ripped away from his thoughts as many hands reached for cooked fish skewered on sticks stuck into the ground around the fire. One grunt from the warrior and all arms disappeared. 'Eleu was to help himself first. Evidently, it was not polite to eat before the guest. He gingerly took a skewer, and then the melee started. Some fish fell apart and bits dropped into the fire, and the stew pot was nearly dumped over, and minor squabbles broke out over lost food. They all managed to retrieve the dislodged fragments and settled into chatter with mouths full of food, accompanied by a dissonance of belching and lip smacking. 'Eleu's tray was filled again, which was fine with him as he was very hungry. But when it came around a third time, he prayed he would not offend by declining especially that awful oil on which he might become sick. Their only drink was water. All ate until they were glutted, and not one bit was left on their trays or even among the coals.

There was some entertainment for their guest. Chanting and dancing with whistles, rattles, and drums began to fill the large cedar-plank house and rose to a fever pitch until the performers, twirling and running in circles, collapsed onto their boxes sweating profusely. The Indians began retreating to their rooms, and 'Eleu began to notice more about his surroundings. The large house was divided into areas for the extended families of the warrior chief. Made of upright planks, they gave a small amount of privacy for sleeping quarters away from the central gathering place.

The chief struck up a one-sided conversation with 'Eleu, talking about many things; but again, the mix of three languages made his head swim, and he was not able to respond. Finally, the chief himself fell asleep right there on his box. 'Eleu had fought the good fight in trying not to be rude by falling asleep on his host, and when he did retire to his bed on the blanket, he covered himself with his bear skin and never thought of another thing.

However, 'Eleu was awakened several times during the night by someone's departure from the house or his own trek out into the black night. Other sounds and movement occasionally disturbed his sleep, but he passed them off as amorous goings-on between men and women. He did not know if he would ever be able to sleep with all the commotion of the crowd inside the house, but sleep he did.

Morning came and the warrior's rituals for the day began. First, it was plucking of facial hair with mussel-shell tweezers. The warrior offered them to 'Eleu, but he declined, causing the man to scowl at the full growth on his new friend's face. Then bear grease and red ocher paint were applied to the warrior's copper-brown face and body in patterns of stripes or squares depending on how his individual mood directed. Men only decorated themselves with the odd combination of ingredients for festivities. Their hair too was heavily oiled and gathered in a bunch on the crowns of their heads held in place with a small leafy branch of a tree, leaves hanging all around. Stuck to the goo was a white substance like snow, powdered all over so as not to leave a spot uncovered. 'Eleu had seen that display before but never applied. He smothered a laugh, not wanting to offend and wanted to know what the white material was. The white down of the bald eagle was the answer.

Women did not have such grand decoration using only black painted moon-shaped eyebrows and one red ocher line going from each corner of their mouth up to their ears. Both sexes wore cedar-bark material draped or fastened about them, belted with leather or bark tie or just thrown about their shoulders.

'Eleu tied his hair back, knotting it with a strip of cloth, and walked out in his skins and moccasins ready to join the hunt with the tribe despite the warrior's pleas to ornament himself.

A man from the king's residence brought him a good-sized bow and a basket-quiver of arrows of superb quality made of unknown wood. They were a gift from the king for saving the life of the warrior. 'Eleu let go an arrow across the compound, aiming for a mere sliver of a tree among the giant red cedars surrounding it. The tensile strength was crisp and perfect, and the arrow whipped by whale sinew whistled across space until the copper point pierced the target with a thud.

One of the Indians jumped for his life, feeling the breeze of the arrow past his ear. 'Eleu smiled and got a nod of approval from the man and the warrior who just stepping out of his plank house was fashionably attired and strutting proudly. He walked over to 'Eleu and corrected his way of holding the bow, horizontally not vertically. The warrior himself let go an arrow piercing the trunk causing 'Eleu's to fall to the ground. It was impressive, but not cause enough to change the way he held his weapon.

Neither the warrior nor the king would be going on the hunt as they were expecting the Yutlinuk tribe from the northeast of Vancouver Island to get a wife for the warrior's son. The Yutlinuk's population was dwindling, and to strengthen his tribe, the chief chose his daughter to marry into the Nootka rather than intermarrying with the neighboring and already related tribes.

The Makah tribe was also invited. They lived one hundred and fifty miles south across the Strait of Juan de Fuca and closely related to the Nootka.

Both king and warrior were garbed in their finest attire for the bartering, and festivities would start as soon as the tribes and hunting party arrived.

'Eleu joined the hunting party of commoners and slaves and spent most of the first day searching for wapiti. The skin of the elk with its soft gray hair called metamelth was of superior quality and very valuable. Prepared and decorated, it was worn only by chiefs as a great war dress or embellishment on other garments. The common man wore scraps tied on wrist or ankle as ornaments, still highly prized. Its meat was for food, its antlers for whaling, and its bones were for making hooks and other useful items. The hunters were blessed with two kills for the day, thanks in part to 'Eleu's help in tracking. Their king would be pleased.

Even though 'Eleu was adept at capturing duck with the line of his pīkoi, that was the slow way of getting some waterfowl. As the long day turned to rain and darkness, 'Eleu was about to learn another lesson. The hunters came upon a lake, and he was handed a torch and warned to be quiet. Suddenly, many torches were lit and stuck into holes in hidden canoes. Many geese and ducks rested on the surface of the water, and although the men paddled out, none of the birds took flight.

Bark nets were thrown over the easy prey, and thirty-three birds were caught in one attempt. 'Eleu was reminded of the night fishing that was done in lagoons at home—many fish caught with many spears. In each case, unsuspecting creatures were dazzled by the light.

The party was put to the test on the second day. It seemed as if the hunted went into hiding. The leader decided it was not worth going after any more prey especially as the rain came lashing down, and they wanted to get their prizes back to camp for the potlatch.

As the men started back, they startled a black burly bear, causing the animal to stand his ground upright at seven feet high. One hunter tripped over a debris-hidden log and was nearly attacked, but when 'Eleu raised his bow on the brink of shooting the bear, several of the men stepped in front of his weapon pleading for him not to kill the animal. They were frightened beyond his understanding, and others of their party shot their muskets in the air to scare it off. It was bad luck to kill a bear in their culture. Killing the animal would send away the fish. 'Eleu had a lot to learn about their culture and religious practices, but he recalled the admiring glances cast toward him in their first meeting when they found his bearskin.

Potlatch and Aftermath

Midwinter 1800, the three tribes were assembled, the hunting party had returned, and a potlatch was to be held. The potlatch ceremony was the dispersal of accumulated wealth by the host, honoring the guests with generous gifts. It solidified bonds of friendship, alliances, and commemorations of important events like the marriage.

All the women were buzzing with excitement about the newest member of the Nootka tribe, about her clothes and ornaments, and about the gifts given by her father to his new son-in-law and most especially to their host, the king. The warrior's son would be in line to take his father's place as second in command under his uncle, the king, and the Yutlinuk and Nootka would forge a cultural and political bond.

The boxes in the houses of the king and chiefs were opened and hundreds of prime otter, seal, and beaver skins, and metamelth hides were piled in the middle of the compound along with woven blankets, hats, baskets, and decorated whorls for looms.

All meat and fowl were cooked. Dried salmon, cod, halibut, whale blubber, clams, and herring spawn were laid out before the throngs of tribal members at least three thousand strong. Gallons of oil procured from last spring's whale blubber were provided as sauce for everything. Delicious yama cakes made from dried salal, the blue-colored berry delicacy that was fresh in summer, were passed around.

'Eleu had never seen such a banquet. It was as if the Nootka were disposing of their all-important items of survival. He was directed to help in giving individual pieces to various members of the two tribes especially the Makah.

Suddenly, he was interrupted in his activity as the tribes cleared a circle in the encampment. "You fight," the warrior said in English, leading him to the center of the ring.

'Eleu was dumbfounded by his friend and suddenly wondered if it was the reason they brought him to their camp, to make a spectacle of him and humiliate him.

The Makah pushed a man forward into the ring. 'Eleu guessed it would be hand-to-hand since there were no weapons visible. He flung off his hide shirt noting the placement of shadows on the playing field and cunningly moved so the sun was in his opponent's eyes. The heavily oiled man was not to be fooled though and stepped in to remove the so-called fighter. 'Eleu blocked his punches and tried to land a few volleys, which slid off harmlessly, and 'Eleu found himself in the dirt with a wicked leg kick.

"Ah, two can play at that game!" He threw hands full of dirt at the slippery man, creating a gritty surface for 'Eleu to grab hold. He could then handle him and anticipate the next move, another off-setting kick, but the man fooled him, using his head as a club trying to break the Sandwich Islander's skull. 'Eleu was too fast for him, the heel of his hand came up under the man's nose, breaking it with an awful crunch and knocking him out cold.

The Nootka men strutted on the fringes of the ring, knowing the superiority of their warrior who would face his adversary proudly. The warrior's son stepped out of the crowd with a wicked looking dagger in his hand.

"What is this nonsense?" 'Eleu thought, glancing at his friend with a look in his eyes that asked the question, "Why?" The man wore a look of contempt. 'Eleu went back to the task at hand. "Okay, what's this all about? Am I supposed to lose to this guy? Make him look good in the eyes of his father, the tribes, his wife? Let him kill me?" He shook his head, shedding those questions and waited.

'Eleu reached for his knife and with horror, realized the thing had come out of its sheath. In a flash, his mind went over the preceding fight. "Where is my weapon?" His peripheral vision caught its glint close to where his shirt lay. It must have come away when he took it off.

Quickly, he somersaulted through the dirt, procuring his knife and shirt at the same time. 'Eleu flipped the shirt around his right arm and held his weapon in his left. Metal clashed in the afternoon sun and sweat poured down each combatant. At every turn, 'Eleu outsmarted the man and effectively used his shirt as a shield until the weapons caught in the air, and the man stepped in, flipping 'Eleu on his back. His knife went flying, and the dagger came down. It missed

'Eleu's chest, deflected by the buckskin shirt and penetrated his shoulder instead. The man stepped back. A cheer went up from the Nootka.

'Eleu got to his feet with blood streaming down his arm, hoping the exhibition was done with the warrior's son winning the battle. Not so, two spears were produced. *"Hoka!"* he cursed in disappointment. His worst weapon in the lua training school. He'd tripped over the thing and got a good laugh at his expense from the students back then. He was on guard and shot a prayer to Kū, god of war, to help him in the skirmish. The warrior's son circled around slowly then lunged, and his spear was blocked. "This thing's unwieldy, too long, great for spearing fish. I wish I could use my pīkoi." All those thoughts filled his mind as his friend's son kept lunging at him. He blocked from the air then on the ground. He almost tripped. The young man was good, nimble, and quick, slashing across the space in front of him and causing 'Eleu to jump backward. They crossed shafts several times and tussled back and forth. Tiredness crept in and his arm hurt, but 'Eleu pushed him away, taking the instant to wipe the sweat and hair from his eyes.

The force of the push caused the son to fall backward, and 'Eleu stabbed his spear in the dirt right between the legs of the warrior's son within inches of his manhood.

"'Ānihinihi ke ola. Life is in a precarious position!" 'Eleu shouted. Humiliating the man in front of all.

The father abruptly walked away, and the crowd dispersed, leaving 'Eleu to wonder what he was doing in this awful place. Any respect 'Eleu had garnered at the beginning with the tribe was gone.

The slave girl tenderly bound up his wound, smiling and patting his arm. He smiled back. A warning bell went off in his head.

It was uncomfortable living in the same house with the two men he mortified before their friends. One evening a few weeks after the potlatch, the slave girl waited on 'Eleu, smiling as usual, but that time, the warrior's son pushed the tray out of her hands, causing it to spill everywhere. Then he kicked her and raised a fist tauntingly. 'Eleu got up and stood between them glaring at the son.

Preferring a slave over a royal one could cost 'Eleu his life, but his friend chided his son and demanded that he return to his wife's side. 'Eleu realized he was in a dangerous situation as the king or the commoners could turn on him at any time. He vowed to get out as soon as possible. He began plotting his escape and stayed away as much as he could without being suspect. He hunted or fished and ate alone, coming back late after all had retired and always watching for any sign of trouble from the Indians.

The next evening, 'Eleu found the men including the king sitting around the fire keeping warm and smoking. He was on the alert, perplexed that they were still awake. The warrior motioned for him to come and smoke with them. 'Eleu sat down and the warrior explained that his brother's wife was giving birth beyond the house in a special place set aside for that purpose. Suddenly, the slave of that woman rushed through the back door, wringing her hands and screaming at the top of her lungs, "The babies are twins!" Faces of stunned surprise stared at her then joyous laughter and dancing followed. All of the good news was lost on 'Eleu. The warrior held up two fingers. "Babies most sacred," he said.

"Māhoe! I have twins," 'Eleu said smiling, happily remembering his family. Celebration turned to awe as the warrior received the news. There in his midst was another sacred father. The new father would be treated with great respect and seated among the chiefs. Their religion taught that twins were salmon children before birth, capable of calling the fish to their spawning grounds. Word of that began to spread throughout the tribe, and within a week, everyone along the coast knew about the wonderful birth and the wonderful visitor at the home of the Nootka. 'Eleu's position in the household changed for the better after the news, but how long that would last, he did not know. He would go on with his escape plans.

For a few months, things went well and the humiliation of the defeat of the warrior's son was forgotten as the tribe had moved and was settling in at their summer camp at Nootka. The whaling season was upon them, and the king asked 'Eleu to join them in a support canoe, an exciting prospect as he had never fished for anything larger than ulua. At home, it was sport for the ali'i to go after niuhi, the great shark, but whaling was something he'd never seen.

The expedition was preceded by the king's trek to a secret place for a day-long prayer vigil, asking the god Quahootze for blessings on the hunt and by another two days, fasting in a dark temper.

Canoes lined the beach with their gear in perfect order: floats, lines, and tow-ropes for the king's inspection. The king's harpoon awaited him in his canoe as only he could strike the whale.

Gray whales, reaching upward of forty-five feet, were seen surfacing on the sea, and the chase was on. The water was swirling around them, and a gust of wind caused the king to miss his first strike. Everyone regrouped and ropes were recoiled. The paddlers had a difficult time maneuvering among the submerging and breaching animals, but when it came time for the kill again, the king threw, and the ten-inch mussel-shell head of the harpoon stuck. Nine feet of whale sinew trailed out while one hundred twenty feet of bark rope played out behind it with the attached seal skin buoys. They kept the animal from diving down and checked its motion.

It was time for the support canoes to do their work. As they got closer, 'Eleu could see the elk antlers holding the harpoon steady on the body of the animal, so it would not come loose from the thick skin. The warrior's son was in another support canoe. With writhing whales, boiling water, and stiff wind, everyone's attention was on the task at hand when 'Eleu was suddenly struck with a glancing blow of a harpoon. The sharp point just missed him, but barbs below the head raked his skin, causing a deep cut under the old potlatch wound. He unbound his hair, using the strip to bind up the wound then scowled at the man who was obviously provoking him to anger.

'Eleu never skipped a beat from his duty though, keeping the lines and buoys from tangling and paddling steadily with the crew to tow the animal slowly back to shore. Keeping it afloat took many hours of back-breaking work. A slow triumphant song was sung by the fishermen, keeping time with their paddles, and the shore people welcomed them back, furiously beating out their joy on the roof planks of the houses. The animal was beached and immediately cut up. The first stripping of blubber went to the king and then to his whaling crew. Everyone else could take what they wanted.

Escape

'Eleu's belongings were concealed in his canoe, hidden carefully down the coast in a small inlet. He was hoping no one would notice its disappearance, and he was careful to place it so the daily bathers would not notice it. The Nootka were a clean people, bathing in the ocean every day. They each had their spot to wash and pray or meditate, 'Eleu could not tell. Some seemed in a trance, but they all had their place.

Unknown to 'Eleu, that day would be his final day with the Nootka. He was out hunting and lost track of the time. It was late when he got back to the camp, some places were lit by large fires. It was Hawaiian pō kāne, an exceedingly dark night with no stars and no moon, a bad time to be out. It was a time for the night marchers at home. One could be killed if one got in their way. One could sometimes see those ghosts carrying their torches as they walked along the ancient trails chanting the ancient oli. It was also a taboo night of the gods Kāne and Lono. It was not a good time to be out. He crawled into his bed, pulling the blanket up around his neck. A chill was running down his spine.

Halfway into his sleep when the central fire of the house was dying down, he felt something lifting his blanket and a presence against his body. It was the slave girl. She always smelled of fragrant herbs or seasonal blossoms worn around her neck or in her hair. She took his arm and draped it over her, cuddling closer to him. Again, the bell went off in his head.

"What is she doing?" He became wide awake and startled to feel a bud of longing. Emotions swirled inside his head. He had felt sorry for her, gone a long time from her family and tribe. Usually being the spoils of war, slaves weren't treated well by many of the natives, and she was no exception. She was obviously very lonely, and 'Eleu had been nice to her. It was natural she would gravitate to him. "But what is she doing?" The tug was getting stronger. His lua training kicked in, holding him with a tight reign of rules dominating his life, and he could not act on the desire that was growing in him. But how he longed for closeness, touch, and enjoyment of the soft body next to him. Relief was not far away, but his brain argued against the natural urges. "My wife, my boys." Whatever he did would affect him the rest of his life and the lives of those beloved ones. He could be a "kāne o ka pō," a spirit husband of the night. A child born of their mating would be sick or die. It would not be far wrong for the girl had been passed around to many of the tribal men who wanted her and to any of the sailors who made their way into Nootka Sound on those foreign ships. He had noticed she was showing signs of maʻi ʻino, venereal disease.

ʻEleu quickly threw off the blanket and crawled away, knowing he was leaving the girl crying. It was the right time. He was gone from the place for good. Out in the dark groping through thick brush, ʻEleu cried and threw up; his face and hands were scratched by the vegetation. He could not see because of the tears of anger and hurt and prayed he was going in the right direction. Stumbling upon his canoe, he thrust off the branches concealing it and pushed out onto the black sea, paddling hard due south and following the contours of the land he had seen and fished. He heard breakers for a distance of about ten miles then they were fainter. He followed the sound, always keeping within earshot. Listening intently, he began heading in a more easterly direction. Finally, paying close attention to the sounds and current, ʻEleu like his ancestors began navigating with his senses. They would not fail him in the dark night.

A faint whisper of dawn sighed in the east, the trees' dark silhouettes jagged against the light. The sea and coast were still black, but ʻEleu paddled unceasingly. At daybreak when the light was on the land, he reckoned he had made at least fifty miles and turned into a small cove where he could sleep and rest. Mindlessly, he pulled the canoe up as far as his exhausted arms would allow and lay down in the sand. Immediately, maka pilau, nasty dream ghosts, pursued and punished him. ʻEleu awoke with the sun straight above him, dazed and more exhausted than when he found the spot.

It was a good place as he looked around, tall trees nearly enclosing a small sand beach. He pulled his canoe further up, covering it with dead branches. There was no tray with hot food handed him by the servant girl. He gagged on his dried fish, thinking of her and what he could have had, and what she would face in the future, forgotten and unloved without the slightest recognition of her as a woman capable of love.

The tree line along the shore was tangled with brush and dead logs that concealed a treasury of wild berries, and he ate freely of them while trying to plod through the debris. Seeing a very tall tree, he climbed, careful of the lower dry limbs that might snap under his weight. From rung to rung, he ascended to the top and saw to his surprise a lake not so far from where he was.

He could also see a large body of water. "Barkley Sound?" he questioned, remembering from years back. Somewhere along the coast, a Charles William Barkley had discovered and explored the area. He was captain of the ship *Imperial Eagle* which had stopped in Hawai'i about 1787. 'Eleu was fourteen then.

The closeness of the water was a good thing, or it could be bad; good to fill his needs, but not good as there were probably Indians in the area.

The task at hand was to decide what to do next. "First thing," he thought, "is my beard. It's got to go." The Nootka had never seen him without it nor had any other tribe, and a smooth face would hide his identity. Using the mussel shell tweezers was trying and not at all comfortable, drawing blood frequently and causing irritation to his skin. He would cut his hair shoulder length as well and wear a cedar-bark garment under his bearskin and the hat of a fisherman to pass himself off as a member of one of the many tribes should an Indian see him at a distance. "Would this work?" he wondered.

Staying in the cove for a few days, he discovered it held many delicious 'opihi, the limpet he loved so much. Prying them off the rocks in the tide pools, he picked out the chewy meat inside and kept the shells with their sharp edges. Other tasty mollusk morsels were also harvested. Those he took back to camp were boiled and eaten or salted and dried. Smiling, he found he'e pali, the tiny young octopus. Trying to bite off the head was always difficult as the small tentacles tickled, grabbing hold up his nostrils. Each one he chose tried to escape in the same way but to no avail. They were just right for the eating.

Blue camas bulbs and red and blue and black berries were there for the taking between his location and the lake. Of the bird bones he'd saved, 'Eleu fashioned fish hooks, going after cod and 'ōpelu, the choice mackerel beloved of his brothers back home. Salmon was easier to catch with his double-pronged spear. Rabbit and other game, he brought down with his pikoi. He salted and dried both fish and game.

He hoped making small fires would not draw any curious natives, but one night, a blood-curdling cry shattered his sleep. Suddenly, a man was all over him with his tomahawk and dagger. 'Eleu kicked him off and then wrestled for several minutes before the man jumped up and disappeared. It was time to leave the cove. Evidently, his disguise didn't work.

'Eleu wanted to head for the Strait of Juan de Fuca[6] having heard there were many inland islands and waterways in that vicinity. Mostly traveling by night and out of sight on the open ocean, he could see fires along the shore. He paddled more leisurely and occasionally in the daytime, skirting the fringes of South Vancouver Island across the strait from Cape Flattery. He was taking a chance, but he would have more luck that way. Allowing himself the happy aspect of

---

6. Strait of Juan de Fuca originally called by the Makah Tribe: ha·č?iq tupał (pronounced hahts'-ik̲ too-puhlth). It means 'the long salt water (ocean)' (per the Makah Museum January 29, 2014).

meeting a ship caused him to smile. He would be prepared for that moment—a tall ship waiting to take him home.

A Ghost

It was not to be however. Finding himself among many islands and spits and capes and peninsulas of land, 'Eleu got lost going from place to place, staying a few days or a week here and there but unable to find his way back to the coast.

It seemed that all the Indian tribes had heard of him and his prowess, and brave warriors would come out of nowhere to test his mettle with short conflicts or longer ones, always ending the same way, they disappeared into the trees. He quit the place and moved further back into the wilderness of land and water.

For many months, no Indian bothered him, but not once did he let his guard down. 'Eleu just survived letting his beard and hair grow again. Occasionally hiding his canoe in some out of the way backwater, he hunted, always searching out higher ground, hills, and mountains and surveying the country around him. He marveled at the vast stretch of waterways on which he looked from his high perch. The country went on forever, north and south. 'Eleu began admiring the many animals he saw—bear, wolf, elk, mountain goat—and some he hunted. He'd seen a cougar once before when he went on the hunt with a shore party from the *Marguerite Anne* but at that time, could not believe that such a large cat existed. He enjoyed tracking them, and once in a while, they tracked him but never bothered to call him a meal. There seemed to be an agreement between them that neither would hurt the other, and there were other hides to be had.

The cold crept back into his bones in the fall of 1800. He wasn't keeping track but was keenly aware of the changing seasons he had never known at home. There they were subtle with slight changes in weather, a smell in the air, the way the clouds looked, and shortened days. But the seasonal times in these coastal areas could be beautiful or brutal or temperamental. And it seemed it was always raining. His longing for home ranked lower than his quest for daily survival every season—for food, clothing, shelter, and vigilance, and he needed the patience for that illusive ship.

Another year passed, and it was always the same, survival, no permanent place to call home, vigilance, and no ship. Anywhere he went, there were more scrapes with lone Indians on or off the trails. He suspected they were always aware of him, watching him, waiting around the next tree dripping with heavy mist or behind a moss-covered stump. The sacred aspect of his existence—knowing he was the father of twins—either caused or discouraged many of them to try him in battle. His reputation more as a god was growing.

Completely unknown to 'Eleu, the ship *Manchester* had anchored at Yuquot and spent the winter of 1801 trading with the Nootka he'd left behind the year before. The ship would go on to do the great triangle in the Pacific Ocean, busily trading wares and dragging crew illnesses from China to the Pacific Northwest Coast to Hawai'i and back again. That trade route changed the way of life for many peoples who had lived in those areas in good health for thousands of years.

Hugging the south side of Juan de Fuca Strait, 'Eleu paddled west toward where he hoped the Makah might be. He rounded a point of land and saw Neah Bay. It was a nice village at the head of a low valley with a river next to it emptying into the Strait. He would eventually find out that the river called Waatch, ran from the Bay to the Pacific Ocean and cut the land in two when the tide was up. Their village and Cape Flattery became an island. 'Eleu was happy for it would be convenient to sight a ship that might be passing into the strait.

The protected leeward peninsula had many calm bays with forested mountains behind. The look of the land was pretty indeed, being completely different than the violent waves of the Pacific Ocean side of the cape. It lured 'Eleu, and so did the Makah people he met at the potlatch. They were friendlier and milder in their manners and fun loving and famous for their singing and dancing. 'Eleu had noted those characteristics at the potlatch as well as the warriors' prowess among the coastal tribes.

When 'Eleu arrived at the Makah village, he stepped out of his canoe, and the people ran in fear to their plank houses. Tribal leaders cautiously approached him as an untouchable ghost. The head canoe maker's curiosity for the well-made canoe with its outrigger, however, outweighed any caution, and he warmly greeted the specter. While the canoe broke the ice with the tribe, the chief decided that a small house away from the village would be made available for his needs.

Compared with the Nootka, the Makah were shorter, but they shared the trait of having deformed feet and legs from sitting on them. Their broad faces and bodies were completely hairless, plucked with mussel shells. An odd mark of high rank was the deformed head produced when, as infants in cradle boards, pressure was applied to the forehead at a thirty-degree angle with the desired effect being a cone-shaped skull.

The Makah's canoes, weapons, and tools were more decorative, and their elk-hide cloth made into clothes was softer, finer, and more beautiful than the Nootka. They also wore beaver fur and the golden skin of a large wild cat. "Hmm," thought 'Eleu, "my old friend, cougar."

The language barrier with the Makah was worse than with the Nootka. Some had learned a little English from trading ships but not enough for 'Eleu to get along. When they had to converse, it was in a sort of sign language. His own language turned inward with constant prayers to his ancestors, providing continuous strands of connection to—and his only tenuous support from—his former life.

In his new home, 'Eleu set his adze kit on the ground and removed the canvas bag and the hau wrapper to check his remaining implements—stone-headed adzes, drill, caulking tool, chisels, and clamps. His hammer stones had been lost somewhere along the way. Hau and 'aha were disintegrating in the damp climate. He must get rid of the last vestige of home, but as he began to remove it, the head canoe maker stood over him. He was fascinated by what he saw and knelt down beside 'Eleu, rolling out his own kit wrapped in elk hide. The man picked up the 'aha, marveling at its braided strength but noting its integrity was in question; and he compared it to the cedar-bark cordage the Makah used. Handing 'Eleu a length of rope that was in his hand and using sign he was telling 'Eleu that he would show him how it was made. 'Eleu cupped his hands then spread his thumbs apart, again using sign to ask how they got their canoes so broad. The man nodded his head understanding his new friend. "We will build," he said to 'Eleu.

The man who received the broken nose at the heel of 'Eleu's hand at the potlatch had died while on a whaling expedition the year before. It was time for the tribe to build a new canoe to replace the one that was damaged. The Makah did not make many canoes, mostly because the size needed of red cedar trees that far south were not as prevalent as on Vancouver Island. Trade with the Nootka was preferred. Hunters, however, had come upon several large specimens of trees, and tagged them. The man asked 'Eleu to go along, and his eyes were all over the craft, feeling with his hands the workmanship of the cedar and noting the highly ornamented designs. He surveyed the nohona waʻa and wae that supported them and noted there were no splinters or bits of any kind anywhere on the canoe that had not been sanded away.

Several whaling canoes were employed with six or so natives in each to tow a likely candidate back to camp. A shaman was with them to lead religious ceremonies and bestow the correct prayers on the canoes and ask for a successful venture.

Down the coast and a little inland was the first of the enormous hulks the tribe would examine. ʻEleuʻs mind was boggled by the girth, but the tree was shunned for no reason he could see. His expert eye even without the help of the ʻelepaio bird could tell which koa trees were ripe for the adze, but the practiced eye of the Makah saw something wrong or evil in the tree as their religion dictated. They hiked further, and the other tagged specimen presented itself. After walking around the trunk and eyes scrutinizing every square inch, the man pronounced, "Whale canoe." That would be the one to be sculpted into the proper dimensions. ʻEleu could not ask what their criteria were, so as he did as a little child, he watched and learned. With the use of their stone-headed adzes, the process of bringing down the massive tree was painstakingly slow, taking two days as it did in the Hawaiian way. ʻEleu could see the benefit of iron axes used by the sailors for cutting wood for the *Marguerite Anne*, but there was something to be said about the way things had been done for centuries—with the blessings of the gods. The crack of the trunk was sharp in the deathly quiet of the forest as it fell on its own bed of chips removed by the adzes of the men. Before nightfall, branches and bark were removed and ʻEleu could tell by the satisfaction on their faces it would be good.

Stern and bow were shaped outside and roughly carved inside. Chisels gently tapped along the inside edges of the core, freeing it for the work of the stone-headed hammers and wedges. They were employed at one end, beginning the process of severing a thickness of plank from the center. Several progressively narrower planks were removed in the same way, and the rest was roughly shaped. The hull bottom was flattened, and a channel was cut at point of bow and stern to receive ropes for the craft to be towed through the ocean and back to the village.

The rest of the canoe was hulled out and smoothed. The head canoe maker took it from there. 'Eleu and the others could not watch. It was taboo like many other things of the trip: women, sex, and hair combing. The Makah religious practices were similar to the Hawaiian's. The head canoe maker's job was the widening process, freshwater poured in at a four-finger depth, red hot stones dropped into it by tongs, and hot water sprinkled over the entire surface of the sides. The canoe-in-the-making was also heated by fires from the outside, crossbars gently stretching the sides.

Meanwhile, others were making the decorative bow and stern pieces, carved from a separate log and attached by dowels and lashings, making the seams waterproof. 'Eleu, completely mesmerized, stood at the shoulder of the man doing the lashings. The process was not much different than his training, and suddenly, the man stepped aside and let 'Eleu try. Stunned, he hoped he would not be all thumbs. The man pointed out a special twist and tie that 'Eleu caught on to immediately. He was given a nod of approval. It seemed as if the fear of him was being dispelled by his canoe-making expertise.

Beautiful carvings of eagles were created on both pieces, and painting the canoe inside and out using seal oil and red ocher gave the canoe a fine-looking appearance. The shaman chanted prayers of thanksgiving for the beautiful whaling canoe that was floating in the water as he spoke. A celebration followed with admiring eyes and hands touching the smooth surfaces of the exquisite craft. The whole of the process had taken many months with many hands.

Three years went by in the bay of the Makah. 'Eleu was very much by himself and came and went as he pleased, but they treated him well especially as he shared with them whatever he took from the sea and forests around them, and the Makah shared potatoes—white fingerling potatoes— brought by the Spanish fifteen years before when they attempted a colony at Neah Bay. The settlement was abandoned, but the potatoes stayed behind.

In the early summer of 1804, 'Eleu had wandered far afield. One day, he found something familiar, two very tall twin pine[7] trees. The trunks reminded him of a tree talked about in Waimea on his home island when he was a child. He was with his great-grandfather in the men's hale when the Kīpuʻupuʻu warriors talked about the pine-log flotsam washed up on Kauaʻi Island's shore. The canoe made from that log was very famous in all the islands.

'Eleu had an idea. He walked around the two trees and thought, "If they are perfect, what a fine double-hull canoe they would make." He looked at the angle of the ridge and at the fast moving stream at the bottom. "Yes, I think it could be done." The branches grew lower down on one of them, and he climbed, examining both trees. The diameter looked right, and the length would easily accommodate the platform in between the hulls. He would need mats for the sails. The Makah mats for their ocean-going canoes were not as fine and strong as the Hawaiian, but he thought they would do until a ship came along to provide them with the canvas needed.

---

7.   Oregon Pine or Coast Douglas Fir

'Eleu was delighted with his idea, and there was enough time to carry it out before the cold set in and snow fell. He went back to the village and told the head canoe maker about the plan. Would he and some of the canoe makers like to come and allow 'Eleu to show them how Sandwich Islanders make their canoes?

A temporary shelter was the first concern. The men would be on the ridge for several months and would need a snug place to eat and sleep.

Again, 'Eleu tested the two trees. In his reckoning, they were each about two hundred feet tall and about fifteen feet in girth. His voice had not left him over the years, and he sang out his oli to the appropriate gods then he lifted his prayers to his mother to help him. He had no proper gifts of black pig or red kapa or any of the treasured verdant greens to give, but he knew the gods would not mind considering the circumstances.

'Eleu began by dividing the work force into two groups. Each would remove the back branches of each tree. Those limbs were then laid behind as a bed for the trees to fall on. Digging around the pine's base up slope of the tree, the roots were removed. From fallen logs he had seen, 'Eleu thought their root system was minimal and wanted to let them fall the shorter distance up slope. Day after day, he worked like a man with the goal of a lifetime and directed the Makah in the Hawaiian art of canoe making.

Eventually, both trees were down without even a crack, and they were perfect. Stripped of bark and partially hulled out, they began tying them off and placing one man at the bow of each log for steerage with their feet while the others held the heavy wood with lines. The men began to enjoy what they were doing as the grass-covered ridge allowed the logs to go quickly but steadily downslope. It was just a matter of towing the two hollowed-out logs behind two of the tribe's large whaling canoes and paddling them back to the village.

When they arrived, the tribe was amazed and bewildered at the sight of the two large logs. What were their brothers going to do with those gigantic pieces? Even the king could not believe his eyes.

It was a grand scheme. 'Eleu had not been sure if the Makah would take to the idea of creating something new. All of their men were skeptical at the start, but as time went on, they were able to see the logic. "Why the two canoes?" he could read in their faces, but when the hulls were finished and the platform was attached, 'Eleu could show them the purpose. He had calculated the completion to coincide with the move to their spring camp for whaling season.

Like the Nootka and all the tribes living along the Pacific Northwest Coast, the Makah had several camps for each hunting or fishing season. Living in houses made of red cedar planks, it was easy to remove the planks and take them to be set up on the foundations already in place in the next camp. The Makah struggled with moving house planks from Neah Bay around Cape Flattery south to Ozette Lake for the whaling season. 'Eleu's platform on the double hulls could manage much more weight than a single dugout, carrying a few cedar planks at a time or three of them lashed together carrying many planks crosswise. With the sides flared out on the canoes, it was impossible to keep the hulls straight with the shifting weight, causing their scheme to fail with the load landing in the ocean.

'Eleu had moved away from the Makah, wandering south along the coast and always watching for the sail that would salvage him from his exile. They had told him about a large river to the south that might be promising for a trading ship, so he pressed on. But at night, he sat with the only warmth he knew, awash with fading memories. Sadness was replaced by numbing emptiness.

Coals, tumbling around or collapsing into heaps of gray ash, crackled and split throwing out sparks reminiscent of the molten lava of his home. He threw a small branch into the mix. It popped and released a swirl of smoke into the treetops. Staring at the scene, he pulled a stick from the fire and lit his pipe, drawing in the rich flavor of the tobacco. Sitting cross-legged, he reminisced about how he'd come by that tobacco in the little bag.

Hiding in a seaman's chest among the salvage of the wrecked *Marguerite Anne* was a small wooden box containing a tobacco pouch with a sweet-woodsy fragrance. He'd smelled it on the sailors during the voyage, but the tide was rising, causing the destroyed ship to list, so he thrust it in with his adze kit, thinking it might come in handy at some future time, and forgot about it.

When 'Eleu's hau wrapper and binding of 'aha containing the adze kit given to him as a wedding present from Kahikina's parents finally rotted away, he fashioned a new one with elk hide, making pockets and adding ties. While transferring his tools into the new wrapper, he noticed the treasure jammed in a corner of the disintegrating woven mesh. During his time with the Nootka, they gave him a smoking pipe, but he never cared for the bark they smoked. Suddenly, his newfound discovery was very satisfying, keeping him company in desperate times or sad spaces between work and sleep.

'Eleu slowly let go the smooth aromatic smoke from his nostrils and mouth, watching it combine with flames and sparks from the fire. He remembered the word Virginia where the sailors told him the tobacco was grown. He repeated it out loud, startling himself, "Virginia." "Wonder where that is? Someplace in Boston?" He shrugged and his thoughts evaporated in the smoke, but a memory lingered, a scent of maile or 'iliahi or laua'e.

Off in the distance, an 'ohe, reminiscent of a nose flute, caught his attention. It was played by a lonely hunter or one of a group of Indians sitting around their campfire as 'Eleu was doing. He had heard the pipes before, the music was sweet, melancholic, and dreamy. The tune continued, enkindling his mind with memories of nights he'd thought he'd left behind, he at five years old safely in front of his parents' sleeping hale and listening to lovers calling; in the forests of Waimea after the felling of the canoe tree with his great-grandfather Ka'ōka'i; his beautiful wife's soft body and twin babies tenderly rocked to sleep; after work in the peleleu camps with his friend Waipā; on board the ship with his friends Jack, Tom, and Billy. His heart nearly burst with sorrow remembering those losses. He put the pipe down and ached for love, for touch, for affection, for compassion.

Loneliness stripped him bare as a knife cutting away his very soul and carving his body in pieces like Hawaiian burial preparation of removing skin, sinew, and muscle, and folding up skeleton, wrapping it, and putting it in a dark place. Depression wrapped him in a smothering shroud. He never felt so far from his home than he did at that moment. "Should he give up? Should he forget his wife and family and create a new life in this far distant place?" He could not. His family, his culture, and his 'āina were too important to him. Oh, the agony he felt.

A small group of Clatsop Indians called on him in the morning. His fire had gone cold, his pipe had gone cold, and his cold heart was still asleep. They came bearing fish and game as friends and called out to him.

He was like a ghost to them, someone who could take care of himself and one who could fight and kill if necessary but was seemingly never to be touched. His fame was renowned on the coast. No man could ever approach him in that manner with his guard down. They thought about it, and 'Eleu awoke with a start, weapon in hand. They stepped back in fear. 'Eleu relaxed when he saw his friends, never knowing what had been in their collective minds.

One dared to ask, "Would you come to our newly-acquired home on the south shore of the wide Columbia River?"[8]

"Yes," the big Hawaiian man told them.

---

8. The Columbia River is called *Wimahl, Nch'i-Wàna* or *swah'netk'qhu* by various Indian Nation peoples living along its banks. All three terms essentially mean the big river. In 1792, it was named the Columbia River by Gray. Clarke says that, in 1805, the Indians knew it as the Shocatilcum or Chockalilum.

SPRING (1806)—GOING HOME

'Eleu caught salmon early one morning. They were big and fat, and their orange flesh was succulent when broiled over the coals or salted for carrying on the trails. And they lasted through winter. He tossed pieces of dried salt salmon and black berries into his mouth then ate a yama cake, washing it down with water. He paddled lazily along a small tributary on the south side of the Columbia River, checking his traps. Brushing away a low hanging branch, a cloud of dead leaves descended over him and his canoe. "Dead like my heart," he thought.

It was mid-May and spring was upon the land of New Albion, which belonged to the English and was situated between the Russians to the north and the Spanish to the south. Given the bounty of the area, he and his Indian companions could begin to prepare to survive the winter again, but he was horribly lonely and had given up finding a ship to go home. His family had become a dim memory.

At Ft. Clatsop, 'Eleu arrived with a canoe full of fish and game, and the Indians gave him a look of approval as they swiftly emptied the hull. The canoe had held many loads since he had made it six years before. Preparations were already underway for the evening meal, and the canoe maker's son, already thirty-three years old, was hungry, hungry for many things.

After Meriwether Lewis and William Clark and the Corps of Discovery had abandoned their fort in March of 1806, the Clatsop tribe had inherited and occupied the structures. 'Eleu had come to the fort in early spring with his Indian friends. The rest of the tribe welcomed him to their new dwellings. He ate with those savages so called by the sailors of the *Marguerite Anne* and tried to listen to the campfire talk, knowing a little of their language. What savages meant, he never knew as the Indians seemed to be not much different than his own kind, sometimes good and sometimes bad and just with different ways of surviving depending on their surroundings. They desired love and companionship as all men did.

There was a cold in the air that night as if winter did not want to leave. It got into their bones, causing the tribe to move closer to the fire and pulling their fur robes tighter around chilly shoulders. Many wandered off to their beds in one of the structures, and some merely fell off into a deep sleep right where they were. As it started to rain, 'Eleu went to his corner in one of the buildings of the compound. There were no more maka pilau in his dreams. In fact, there were no more bad dreams at all. There was just hard work to exist day after day before falling into heavy exhaustive sleep at night.

There had been ships coming into the mouth of the Columbia but none for many moons as related by the Indians. When asked, they only gave Lewis and Clark a list of the men, not ship names. The Corps needed supplies, which had been promised from their mentor President Jefferson but none ever came.[9]

Before the light of day, 'Eleu awoke to noisy loud snoring, gathered up his belongings and walked through the courtyard of the fort. All was gray in the early dawn; the fire had all but gone out. A wisp of gray smoke rose from gray ash. Bits of salmon bones and rabbit fur were scattered from the night's dinner. Even the dogs were not aroused by 'Eleu's passing except for one who raised his head with some of that rabbit fur clinging to his muzzle. He sneezed and seemed surprised to see a tiny cloud of fur waft about his nose. But he was not at all curious about the big man and immediately went back to sleep. The large fortified gate to the compound opened and closed softly, and 'Eleu walked silently to the water's edge and waiting canoe.

'Eleu paddled up the creek and out of the mouth of the Columbia River alone. He had a little difficulty navigating the pounding surf. It was seventeen miles from Ft. Clatsop to the salt-maker's camp at Tillamook Head, and 'Eleu never knew that Lewis and Clark's men had made that same trek just a few months earlier. There were violent seas over the sandbars at the river mouth that could cause lost canoes and dead men if one weren't careful. Going south, the shore was fairly straight but the wind was blustery. Reaching the salt-makers-camp, a warm memory surged through 'Eleu as he surfed his canoe onto the beach just as he had done when he was young.

---

9. The ship *Lydia* sailed ten miles up the Columbia River passing the Washington shore late Nov. 1805. The Corps had already moved seven miles south to where Ft. Clatsop was built. The inhabitants of the village told Capt. Hill that Lewis and Clark were there, but neglected to tell the Corps the *Lydia* had come and gone.

The camp consisted of a temporary shelter from the frequent storms and a low rock wall enclosing an oven of stones. Tillamook Indians had permanent dwellings a short distance away and were there tending kettles of seawater boiling over a driftwood fire that would make excellent salt. With sign language, they acknowledged 'Eleu's presence by pointing to some buckets. He laced the buckets' ropes over the pole and lifted them over his shoulders behind his head. Coming back, the load was full with sloshing water and was considerably heavier. Hāhāpaʻakai, getting salt at home was much easier when his mother took him to Laeʻapuki south of Kapaʻahu on Hawaiʻi Island. One could scoop it up out of holes in the sea-washed lava plain.

He stayed a few days with the men, helping obtain and boil sea water and putting the residue salt out to dry, which was always difficult along the rain-swept coast. With his efforts, and by trading some blue beads and many buttons, he managed to get twenty pounds of salt. Fortunately, the weather had been fairly clear and dry.

'Eleu was satisfied with his success but happy to be on his way. Within ten miles, he paddled into a thick fog, causing him to lose sight of the coast. He could hear the pounding surf on the shore and tried to keep the sound of the waves within earshot, struggling through the treacherous sea with his broad paddle. Hours went by, but he lost the sound of the surf, thinking he had made it to the mouth of the river. However, the fog dissipated quite as suddenly as it had come.

He looked east and discovered he was off course by at least and mile and a half. At that same instant, he heard another sound to the west of his position, voices! 'Eleu turned his head and could not believe his eyes. A three-masted ship was within less than a quarter mile of his position, sailing south. He could actually see the American flag flying at the stern. He paddled as fast as he could and was spotted by an officer looking at him through the glass. 'Eleu could hear the command given to the topmen to reef the sails.

Waving frantically, he came alongside saying in the best broken English he could muster, "Permission to come aboard, sir?"

Jonathan Winship captain of the *O'Cain* with a very surprised look on his face said, "Permission granted."

Sailors threw down ropes, and 'Eleu swung himself dexterously up to the steps on the side of the ship. A shrill cry pierced the sky and interrupted his ascent. He stopped mid-step and saw a very large bird with a seven-foot wingspan soaring high above—the bald eagle. It banked and flew low over the water's surface, grasping a fish with it talons in mid-flight. 'Eleu finally saw his "big bird with the enormous wingspan."

The captain commanded the canoe to be salvaged, and some crew repelled over the side for the prize, which they needed. It was heavy with bags of salt and unwieldy 'iako and ama, and 'Eleu's belongings. 'Eleu's eyes swept the crowded deck and saw native men and women and white men on board, including some Lukia—Russians—wearing their distinctive black fur coats and hats. His heart leaped with joy as among the crew were men of his own kind, nine kānaka on the heavily laden ship. Heavily laden because they also carried many native canoes stacked on the deck, and he guessed, below decks as well.

"And who are you?" the captain asked of the tall man standing before him dressed in skins and fur. 'Eleu had not talked to a white man in a very long time and tried to talk in a mixture of English and Hawaiian.

He stammered in English, "My name...Louie... No...'O 'Eleu ko'u inoa, He Hawai'i au. My name is 'Eleu, and I am Hawaiian!" He was happy to hear himself speaking his native tongue. The astonished kānaka, not recognizing the stranger behind the heavy beard, circled around him, all speaking at once to their brother.

The *O'Cain* left Boston October 7, 1805, sailing around Cape Horn in January 1806. On March 30, they were in Hawai'i and took on board nine Sandwich Islanders as supplementary crew and George Clark as third officer. Clark left the trading ship *Pearl* and had been living in the islands. His reputation as a good seaman was known by Captain Winship. They spent most of April at sea and sighted Sitka on the twenty-third, which was a thriving Russian settlement at Norfolk Sound. 'Eleu remembered seeing a Russian there in 1799.

"I was up there six years ago on the *Marguerite Anne*," 'Eleu said, using the kānaka as interpreters. The officers standing around, arms folded, listened to his tale, and rolled their eyes over the tragedy of the wreck of the *Marguerite Anne*, its smuggling customs, and its harsh treatment of sailors.

The Russians had no luck dealing with the Indians at Sitka and joined forces with Captain Winship and the Americans for a successful trading venture and eventual colonizing. There were no European or American settlements from Sitka all the way to the Spanish mission at San Francisco Bay, so the Captain and his officers were astonished at 'Eleu's tale. Even more astonishing was the story of Lewis and Clark on the south side of the Columbia River. Their Voyage of Discovery to find a northwest passage was a secret venture of the United States Government at the request of President Thomas Jefferson, so those men on the *O'Cain* knew nothing of it.

"I was told by the Clatsop there," he said, pointing to the mouth of the river, "that the white men left in March." Again, his words were interpreted. Captain Winship was dismayed that they had totally missed their chance at meeting the famous gentlemen.

'Eleu settled in among his own men and took to doing whatever was asked of him. Again, he swayed in his hammock in the crews' quarters, obeyed the bosun's pipe, and thoroughly enjoyed his sailing adventure with an eye to a future of returning home.

The *O'Cain* was headed to those Spanish settlements. On June 3, opportunity found them trading on shore at Whale Cove just north of Cape Foulweather, a landmark named for its bad weather by Captain Cook years before. Two days later, they were at Cape Orford on the south coast of Oregon. Five days later on June 10, 1806, Captain Winship sent out two boats, searching the shore for a sufficiently large harbor or bay to begin trading. They found the entrance to the Bay of Trinidad so called by the Spanish, in which there was a known village of Indians and many sea otter pelts to be had. Tacking back and forth, the captain finally dropped anchor, and on the morning of the next day, he sent out fifty of the native canoes, one with the Russian supervisor and George Clark commanding the scouting party. They hunted and camped for two days and nights, but the Indians were hostile toward them, so they quit that shore and returned to the ship.

The next day, the ship's long boats were sent out, checking the shore a little farther south. They were in a light misty fog, and as it swirled around, sandbars appeared and an outlet with ocean tides flowing in and out. The crew paddled easily over the sandbars and were in the mouth of a very large bay. But it was not on any chart.

How could a bay seemingly as large as that one not be discovered? A long coastal mountain range ran behind it, and as characteristic of the Pacific Northwest Coast, the place in Spanish California was similarly cloudy and rainy. George Clark surmised that all of those factors were probably the reasons for its absence on any map. It simply was not visible due to the weather and the contours of the land.

There was a note of excitement among the *O'Cain*'s officers and crew that they had discovered something new. Captain Winship named the place the Bay of Resanof[10] for the son-in-law of the founder of the first Russian colony in America, which pleased that Russian supervisor very much indeed. They charted the bay's shoreline and its islands, which were covered with cypress trees. They logged latitude and longitude and depth measurements. They also recorded the wildlife they found: many sea otters, birds, and an abundance of fish and shellfish. Oysters and mussels were plentiful, and the Sandwich Islanders of the party began collecting the bivalve delicacies. Even though their desire was very strong, 'Eleu stopped them as it was summer, and they were poisonous. He had heard from the sailors on the *Marguerite*

---

10. Humboldt Bay

Anne that some members of Captain George Vancouver's crew became ill, and one had died in 1793 enjoying those very morsels. A flock of black Brandt geese came flying in low across the bay to land in a bed of dark green eel grass. Well, they would have to be satisfied with fish and fowl and the delicious limu, the seaweed of the bay. Much time was spent trading with the Indians for the larger California sea otter pelts and other skins.

When not on duty, 'Eleu stood at the railing and watched the coastline of Alta (upper), California go by. He marveled at the land features much different than the Pacific Northwest Coast. It was warmer, and he shed the furs he wore. There were heavily forested areas. There were coastal areas with windswept trees along wild-looking shores. Scrub-brush areas were obviously devoid of rain most of the year. White sandy beaches were backed by high cliffs. But instead of being excited by the Spanish and their settlements at the bays of San Francisco, San Pedro, and San Diego, 'Eleu found it to be tiresome. He wanted to be home and done with the exploration. He stayed aboard ship and found consolation in his dreams.

The *O'Cain* sailed gracefully with good breezes down the coast. It was September 1806, and Captain Winship left a hunting party on the island of Cedros in Baja (lower), California. It was an arid place but rich in sea lion colonies and sea otters, and humans had lived there for many thousands of years. Yellowtail, bass, and sheepshead were plentiful in the kelp-rich waters. He would pick up his men on the way back.

The *O'Cain* made its way to the Sandwich Islands to hire more men to join with the Americans and Russians to work the trade. That was the happiest news of all to 'Eleu's ears. Winship would let him leave the ship when he was ready and wherever he wished.

The days passed quickly, and 'Eleu found himself enjoying the sailing, willingly at work with the ships' company. Only four weeks remained until he reached home. He was a seasoned veteran, climbing like an acrobat through the upper regions of the masts, sails, and ropes. His pale skin was getting color back in the warming sun, and a feeling of hope like the gray smoke rising from the gray ash of that Indian campfire at Ft. Clatsop sparked a small lick of flame within him. He wondered if his family was still in Waimānalo. "Had they waited for him? Were they well? Would they recognize him?" As usual, his head was all jumbled with questions that had no answers.

One day, he recognized a fragrance in the air. The fragrance of home. His heart nearly leaped out of his chest.

Captain Winship stopped first in Kealakekua where 'Eleu's memories were of making the king's war canoes and the terrible agony of being shanghaied. But he also remembered the good times at the lua school. One man was hired on from there and much trading took place and water obtained. The O'Cain's next stop was Lahaina, Maui where the Captain chose only two men from the many Sandwich Islanders clamoring to get on board to make money in the now flourishing fur-trade business.

The last stop was Kākuhihewa, Honolulu Harbor with two more men added to the crew. There was a flicker of recognition and a shared smile between 'Eleu and one of the men as they had worked together at Pāwa'a, making peleleu canoes. 'Eleu took his canvas seaman's bag, carrying his adze kit and the other few belongings he had and in the American tradition, shook hands with Captain Winship and bid him farewell with many thanks.

"Are you sure you won't stay with us, 'Eleu?" the Captain asked, pronouncing his name perfectly as he was used to the language from the many Sandwich Islanders on board.

"We're going to China next year, God willing and would be proud if you would accompany us. All aboard our ship will partake in the bounty we receive from our trade there, and you are a fine seaman."

'Eleu felt honored by the captain's words, but money did not tease him.

"No, I must rejoin my family. It's been a very long time."

Then Winship smiled and wished him "God speed, 'Eleu."

Many months ago, he traded his heavy firs and skins worn in the cold on the coast for cropped pants and a faded striped shirt. In that sailor's garb, 'Eleu climbed down off the ship and onto a long boat. No more would he desire to go on the big ships. He stood in that boat, let loose his waist length hair, and with the wind blowing in his face, felt his great-grandfather, Ka'ōka'i, again turn his head to his future.

In the harbor, which already had a wharf built, 'Eleu saw some canoes preparing for a voyage. He stopped to ask where they were going. Kāne'ohe was the answer. Could he ride with them? "Of course" came the reply. He had long missed the aloha from his home. Around the southeast point of O'ahu, they were coming to Waimānalo, and his stomach knotted. Swallowing hard, he thanked the paddlers and walked across the sandy beach and into the village. Things had hardly changed. Some of the people shielded their eyes from the sun and stared at him. No one recognized him. 'Eleu started to get frightened. "What if..." he thought. The farther he walked, the less he breathed, and suddenly, he came upon his own home. There was a boy working the 'uala, pulling weeds, and replanting shoots that were dislodged from the dirt. The boy looked at the stranger. Another boy came racing around the hale. 'Eleu was stunned. Those were his twin sons; those two babies he cuddled as infants. The three of them stood stark still in the sunlight, looking at each other. He had long hoped his boys did not think that he had abandoned them.

A woman called, "Ānuenue?" No answer. Then called again, "Kahāipo, where is your brother?" When no answer came from either one, she stepped outside the doorway and instantly dropped the water container she carried. In the silence of the midday sun, only the sound of the breaking ipu and splashing water was heard. She had fright written into the lines of her face.

"Kahikina?" 'Eleu said timidly, not daring to breathe. Her fright began to change to recognition.

Covering a smile with her hand, she then took it away saying seriously, "I am not sure who you are, sir." He wondered why. Suddenly, he remembered! He had a full beard and was dressed in sailors clothing.

"Give me a malo, wife," he demanded. She went inside and did as he requested. He put down his gear and left the place. Awhile later, he came back, wearing his wife's best and most beautifully designed malo which had been awaiting his return. His hair was pulled back, and his beard and his ship life were gone.

Kahikina said through her tears, "You look better clean." She flung herself into his arms. She touched the scars on his shoulder looking at him with dismay. They crossed the tattoos and convoluted the indelible design.

"I fear we have both changed, my love," 'Eleu said with longing in his eyes.

"Then we shall start over." He pulled her close and kissed her in a surprising new way, renewing the strand that bound them.

Life returned to the little family. The old great-grandfather had died. Kahikina's brother 'Olu'olu had remained in Waimānalo to care for his sister and two nephews. She told her husband that Waipā had come as promised and told her of the abduction with reassurances that if it were at all possible, he would come back to her. She never doubted. When asked she said, "I just knew."

When 'Eleu left, his wife was just a girl. She had become a mature woman, rounded and beautiful in all the right places. And the boys, they were shy at first, but eventually, it was as if 'Eleu had never left. Kahikina had kept his spirit alive for them. He did everything with them, including teaching them all the old ways and some new ones learned on his adventures in the Pacific Northwest. Of course, they never tired of hearing the stories begging him, "Tell it again, makua kāne. Tell it again!" 'Eleu left out the bad stuff though.

BACK TO KAPAʻAHU

"I must go," he said.

"But why?" Kahikina pleaded. "You've only been home such a short time."

"I have to find out about my father."

After a moment's reflection she said, "Then I will go too, and the boys. But will there be anyone who can remember back that far? That was…"

"Twenty-seven years ago," he completed her sentence. "We shall see…" ʻEleu's voice trailed off as if trying to convince himself that anyone old enough to remember would still be alive.

The little family packed up their beautiful canoe that Kanewa had made with the hope that the trip to Kapaʻahu would bring answers to ʻEleu's mind. Kahikina's brother ʻOluʻolu would not let them go alone. Some friends of his ʻŌnohi and Kahulamu, who had been warriors with Kamehameha, had taken up residence in Kailua during the replenishing of Oʻahu. They had a strong desire to return to their home of Hawaiʻi Island. ʻOluʻolu and his two friends and ʻEleu and Kahikina would paddle, and the boys were placed in between to bail.

It was a difficult stretch crossing the Kaiwi Channel to Moloka'i; the five adults were struggling to keep a straight course against wind and currents. 'Eleu was surprised and proud of his wife, keeping pace with them and amazed at her strength. But he needn't have worried as 'Olu'olu had taught her well while his brother-in-law was gone.

It took a half day to reach safe haven at Hale o Lono where the ancestors built a place of prayer to the god Lono for rain and good crops. There was a small fishing village in the vicinity, and the kama'aina received them with aloha.

Their next destination was Lahaina. A friend of Kahulamu and a former warrior of Kamehameha lived there, and again, the group was received with food and rest and given a name of someone they should see at Kaupō, their next stop. While the men and boys ate their meal, Kahikina, who was eating with the women, marveled at the large village and the people's ability to carve out beautiful farms from the very dry ʻāina. The mountains were at a distance, but streams watered the crops below. They feasted on moa, poi, and limu and chattered like the hens in the yard. At night, each traveler fell into a deep sleep.

Early morning of the third day had them skirting the coast outside the shore break not so close as to be capsized while using the swells to propel them along Maui's east coast through the Alalākeiki Channel. It too was a rough crossing. They did not find the man at Kaupō and continued on to Kīpahulu.

It was a beautiful area with forests above on the eastern slope of Haleakalā, waterfalls, and pools filled with little moi. Spending time with the villagers, they were advised to wait and have their ʻai with them, enjoying the food and the spontaneous entertainment that would follow. The people danced hula for them, and later around a large fire, the men competed with each other to see who could create the best oli for the visitors. The boys fell asleep immediately after eating and even when prodded, could not stay awake for the festivities. ʻEleu's head kept bobbing, and his sore body desired sleep. But he would not be rude to their hosts and forced himself to stay awake.

The next morning, the local men advised waiting to receive sign from the worst channel of all, the ʻAlenuihāhā. It was difficult to cross at best and nearly impossible on days that saw fierce northeast winds. It was good that they waited. The boys were able to swim in the pools, and the men went hunting. They needed the rest.

Even though the villagers wanted them to stay, the portents were good, and the little company left in the calm of the fifth morning. Their faces were tense, however, as they shoved off from the friendly people. An old man chanted a prayer for their safe passage, and it stayed in ʻEleu's mind as the steersman ʻOluʻolu pushed off from the beach. Loaded with fresh food and water, paddles went into the sea, and ahead of them lay the notorious crossing.

The day was beautiful with clear blue sky and light breezes ruffling the waves, but they could not rely on appearances. The paddlers knew what treachery the channel could hold. 'Eleu's mind kept repeating the old man's oli in time with his paddling. Each accented phrase corresponded to the pull of his paddle, and it was easier to keep himself from getting so tired.

As he inhaled for the next phrase, he could smell a change in the air. He looked east and saw to his horror a turbulent build-up of clouds. Forcing him to the present was the steersman's paddle-tap twice on the hull of the canoe, calling for a rest of two paddle strokes. Again, the rhythmic strokes started with their backs straining. Hawai'i Island loomed in the distance. The depth of the channel and the current and winds conspired against anyone who dared to cross it. All eyes were on the east, and another double tap called another rest. The wind picked up. White caps began to show on the waves.

"I mua!" shouted the paddler-steersman, and all on board picked up speed, moving forward on the sickening sea. 'Eleu's face showed concern, and Kahikina was frightened. Her husband could not look back with reassurances, but in her mind's eye, she saw his eyes filled with love for her and so steeled herself to the task of ignoring her fear.

The cumulonimbus clouds were churning, eating up the sky. The east wind began in earnest. Northeast swells, which had been about five feet, were now fifteen feet high and growing larger. The sea suddenly turned white, as did the paddlers' knuckles. Arms and backs were fatigued, and the twins, afraid of drowning, were bailing as fast as they could. Whimpers came from their lips but no one could hear nor comfort them. The wind was deafening. Their only hope was their parents.

The sky turned black, and the canoe was awash in the wild weather. Waves turned into chasms, and it seemed as if wind gusts were coming from every direction. The canoe took a nosedive into a canyon of water but miraculously came up on the other side. Everyone was wet and cold. Their sweat was washed away by seawater and driving rain. Again, they were unwelcome guests in another monster canyon of waves, and again, they were saved and emerged on the other side.

Hours went by in the brutal sea and sky, but the band of intrepid paddlers endured, and quite suddenly, the rain stopped and moved over the green slopes of Kohala Mountain. 'Upolu Point was seen in the distance, and it turned warm even though the wind was still strong. Steering the canoe around the tip of the island, the going was easier, and they all immediately became aware of their exhaustion. They would find a haven to rest before reaching Kawaihae.

Just as the steersman guided the canoe onto a good-sized swell to reach a small bay, there was a man on a surfboard, smiling and riding the wave right alongside them to the black sand beach. Two men had seen them coming from the cliff overlooking the channel and greeted them when the canoe touched the sand. The paddlers could hardly stand when they stepped out of the canoe, and the three local men immediately assisted them to bring it to rest. Kahikina collapsed, and the surf rider immediately went to her aid.

'Eleu had not seen the faces of the men yet; his eyes were stinging from the salty sea spray. He was not even aware of the place where they stood. When his wife collapsed, he tried to fight the man, wishing to carry her himself. 'Olu'olu stopped him and gave him water to clear his eyes. They all drank deeply from those ipu given them by the strangers and splashed water in their faces to cleanse their salt encrusted lashes.

After a few minutes, 'Eleu came out of his stupor and handed back the water gourd. It was only then that he could see the men who came to their aid. Those were the royal messengers who took him to the king's navy yards first at Pāwaʻa and then to Kealakekua to build those peleleu canoes. He realized where they had landed, Honoipu, the famous fishing and surfing spot of the Kohala aliʻi and very close to King Kamehameha's birthplace.

'Eleu dropped to the ground in front of them, asking pardon for their encroachment on the royal lands. The others did so as well.

"Our aliʻi nui is not here. He has resided on Oʻahu for many years now. We watch and protect the land and the royal ones who live here occasionally. They come and go as they please. All of you are welcome as the king's great warriors, and we are happy to see you. If he were here, he would praise your efforts in crossing the great channel." They were kind to 'Eleu, his wife, and twins, remembering the sorrow they caused from ripping him from his home and family there on that beach of Waimānalo.

The little family and their good paddlers were treated well, and the next morning, water and gifts of food were given from those men's own families. They helped launch the canoe and wished the voyagers well on the next leg. The men had not asked nor did 'Eleu reveal the reason for the trip.

Honokoa was a small shallow bay at the mouth of Waipāhoehoe stream just north of Kawaihae. They anchored the canoe and tied it to a stout tree. 'Eleu wished to honor the iwi (bones or resting place) of Kaʻōkaʻi, the great-grandfather who raised him. He shared stories of his childhood with his family and companions. Kahikina listened intently to her husband but gazed around, storing in her memory the contrasts of the dryness of the area and the green tree-covered mountain in front of them with the beautiful blue sea behind.

'Eleu continued giving a history lesson to his sons about the mountains they could see and the great heiau of Pu'ukoholā. Built by the king, Pu'ukoholā looked like a great whale sitting on a hill and the final demise of that rebel king Keōua Kū'ahu'ula sixteen years earlier. Kahikina shivered. She knew the significance of a luakini heiau—a place of sacrificial death.

Her concentration was broken, however, by a man coming down the hill toward them. She touched 'Eleu's arm in mid-story. He turned and shaded his eyes. The walk was familiar, taller than he remembered, but when the man opened his mouth and spoke, tears fell. It was his own friend Wai'aha. What a wonderful gift.

"Where have you been keeping yourself all these years, e ku'u hoa pili ē, my dearest friend?" They fell into each other's arms. Wai'aha's eyes took in the picture of the little family and the paddlers. Introductions were made.

"And these two look just like you. And your beautiful woman? Ah, you were lucky, 'Eleu."

"Where have you come from? Are you living in the same place?" 'Eleu had so many questions.

"You will come to my home, and we will talk." On the way, Wai'aha told them that he had taken over Ka'ōka'i's home at Kawaihae Uka at the old man's request before he died. He was still making canoes although the trees were becoming fewer, and he had to travel farther to get them—all the way to the slopes of Hualālai. They arrived at the old homestead of Ka'ōka'i, which flooded 'Eleu with fond memories.

"My wife told me to go down to the burial place for remembrance this morning. I was in the middle of carving a new canoe and told her I could not leave my work. She is a seer, one of the gifted ones, and she gave me that look. I knew then I needed to go, and there you were."

Wai'aha's wife was older than him, but they were successful in having children and seemed very happy. The two families and their friends ate and talked, and the children played together, but the time for parting came all too soon.

"We must depart for Kailua in the morning. There is an urgency about this trip, and each day, it becomes a more powerful force pulling me home to Kapa'ahu. It will take many more days to get there." His face showed the worry that they would not make it in time. Wai'aha understood him well. He had learned much from his seer-wife.

"You will make it, hoa pili, but don't be surprised at what you find there."

As they turned to go down the mountain slope to their canoe, Wai'aha's wife stepped forward, took Kahāipo's face in her hands and said softly to him, "You are a kahuna kilokilo. Use it well, little one."

"A kahuna kilokilo?" 'Eleu pondered what that might mean as the hours went by in the canoe.

They made good time from Kawaihae to Kailua and its royal center and landed at the small beach of La'aloa just north of the royal center at Kahalu'u. Both centers had been there since the ancient days of King 'Umi. La'aloa was a white-sand cove lined with coconut trees. Lush and verdant slopes beyond, planted by King Kamehameha himself. It was very lovely to the eyes. One of the paddlers, Kahulamu, was born there. He had been gone for twelve years and was being returned to his family by the wonderful strangers. The old kūpuna ran to him, smothering him with honi and chanting his praises with tears falling and arms stretched to the sky.

"Our lost one has returned. He is to be praised," one sang. Another chanted in a decrepit voice, "All the ancestors rejoice that he has been restored to us." Still another wailed,

"The flower, long closed, has opened its petals and released its glorious fragrance."

The old ones kept repeating and repeating until their voices grew hoarse, and they only stopped when the visitors were asked to sit and eat with the whole village. After the meal, the boys went off to play with the local children, and the elders quizzed their returning son and visitors until it was too dark to see. The old ones fell off to sleep right where they were.

In the cool of early morning, 'Eleu's family began loading up again, and Kahulamu stood with them ankle-deep in small wavelets washing the shore. He thanked them profusely, and his heart ached as he let them go especially his friend 'Olu'olu. He felt bad that there was one less paddler to assist them in their journey. A full day of paddling was ahead, and they pushed off on their way to Miloli'i with the name of one of Kahulamu's friends to visit and be refreshed.

Seven miles into their trip was the great bay of Kealakekua, another royal center for many great kings of Hawai'i and the first landing of the first foreigner to Hawai'i's shores, Captain James Cook. There was much history there and of course, the great lua school of Kekūhaupi'o.

'Eleu was going to bypass the bay altogether, but he thought better of it, rounding the point at Ka'awaloa. His twins had heard the stories of how their father had seen the great ships and were thrilled with that added stop. The bay was still a busy place with many ships coming and going, giving and taking. 'Eleu's head and heart were swimming with mixed memories of joy and happiness, anger and loss. But it had become a friendlier place as they were greeted with smiles and waving from sailors on ships to fishermen in canoes. He steered toward Ke'ei to the school he loved anchoring along the rocky shore.

The lua school was still going strong even without its great leader who had fought alongside his hoa pili and adopted nephew Kamehameha at Nuʻuanu Pali. Kekūhaupiʻo had died some years later in a freak accident during a mock battle. ʻEleu was warmly welcomed by the teachers and students who enjoyed the stories of the great warrior and his father Kanewa. Yes, it was true that even ʻEleu's father had remarkably acquired fame within the lava-rock walls of the great school even though he had fought on the wrong side. The twins were shown around as ʻEleu had been. They were proud of their father as he was showered with questions by the young men. Kahikina and ʻOluʻolu were amazed at the reception given their husband and brother-in-law.

ʻEleu could feel a foreboding in the school though. There were old seers in the recesses of all the islands predicting dire consequences for the old ways of war. ʻEleu could see it when he returned from the Pacific Northwest Coast. The king had not needed the large fleet of peleleu canoes because the Island of Kauaʻi had been given to him without struggle. Also, more and more foreigners were pouring into Hawaiʻi nei. Changes were in the air, but future outcomes he could not see, and he left it to the ʻaumākua and all the deities to protect the people of his native home.

In the late afternoon, they pulled into the pretty fishing village that was Miloliʻi, famous for its plentiful marine life. Their ahupuaʻa stretched up the southwestern slope of Mauna Loa with its deep soil from ancient lava flows. The mountain had been quiet for some time, and the people enjoyed an abundance of choice foods.

Again, the travelers were greeted warmly as they had been in their previous stopovers. The shrinking band of paddlers welcomed the nutritious food given in the spirit of aloha and necessary for the hard work. ʻEleu noticed his wife, losing her luxurious rounded body, was becoming lean and muscular. Even the boys had turned wiry as they had taken over the duties of paddling.

They left Miloliʻi and headed to an area of ocean that was notorious for cross currents coming together from east and west and for capricious winds. Those elements combined could be deadly. It was said the *originals* came to Ka Lae first and saw the runs of the big fish the Polynesians relished; however, there were no reefs, few beaches, and just tiny coves. Maybe they had resided at Punaluʻu with its beautiful black sand beach or Waiʻōhinu with its lush vegetation, both royal centers of the Hawaiian monarchs. Only speculation remained as to where they first landed.

Fortunately, the sea was mindful that they were bringing home one of its native sons and allowed them to pass without incident. It was an easy twenty-five miles around Ka Lae, the south point of Hawaiʻi Island to their landing at Honuʻapo.

ʻŌnohi lived close by in Nāʻālehu and had been a distant cousin of Nuʻuanukapaʻahu, a chief of Kaʻū. That man had been a rebel to King Kalaniʻōpuʻu and sorcery through a shark's attack had been the cause of his death. They were welcomed as usual with aloha and a history lesson lovingly sung by the district's people which made the journey easier to bear.

Another day of hard paddling took them along Kaʻū's eastern coast, and they were finally on the last lap of their journey. It was dry, rugged, and volcanic—basalt with a surface layer of ash and cinder mixed with humus in the kīpuka spaces between lava flows. Kalo grew in pockets and ʻuala thrived in the meager soil. Hale and fishing huts on some places along the coast made for a forlorn look about the ʻāina. The residents were hardy folk, scratching out a living as best they could.

'Eleu's family was tired, but seeing Lae'apuki Point where the local people collected salt, he knew they were nearly there.

If anyone was at the paepae wa'a, the canoe ladder at Kī, he would chance it. He had known those people as Kapa'ahu was just a short walk away. He remembered his mother launching this very fishing canoe off that ladder when he was five years old. It was an ingenious device to get a canoe off or land on the top of a twenty-foot high pali. Without it, fishermen with a catch for the many 'ahupua'a in the area would have to travel all the way to Kalapana then they would have to take the fish back to them—a round trip of five miles.

But the ocean was fairly calm, and the swells were not enough to get the canoe up to the point where the local people could help land the craft. 'Eleu was waved off while he back-watered the canoe. He looked with concern at his family as they held their position with the paddles. Finally, he lifted his paddle in farewell to the people then dipped it into the sea for the final distance to Kalapana.

'Eleu picked up a wave and rode the canoe into the small bay, landing perfectly on the beach. The inhabitants saw it coming and ran to the sand. A crowd had gathered. 'Eleu and his family were welcomed with open arms even though there was no recognition in the eyes.

Someone said, "Aloha kāua!" in greeting. "Who do you look for, tall man?" he asked.

'Eleu scanned the crowd. "Aloha kākou! I search for the family of Hōkūpa'a."

An older woman stepped forward out of the crowd. "I am Hōkūpa'a."

"I am 'Eleu, your nephew." He got a lump in his throat as he thought, "She looks just like her."

"Kamahinaohōkū was my mother." She threw her arms around him, and the two held to each other for a long time.

Recovering herself, she saw the four bedraggled ones with him. "Come and eat and refresh yourselves at my home." She gathered them as a mother hen to her chicks, and there was a buzz about the area that a kama'āina, one of their own, had returned.

Again, there was catching up to do, but Hōkūpa'a could tell that her nephew was on a mission. "I will have my son, your cousin, go with you but after a night's rest."

The next morning, 'Eleu told his aunt he would come back and the two would talk more. His cousin was his own age, and the five of them walked the distance to the one who could tell him about his father.

The kalo and 'uala patches were filled with weeds and the hale, which had become run down, was still there, but the old man was on his porch, rocking back and forth in a newfangled foreign-made chair. He saw the people arriving on the trail, and as if it were yesterday, called, "E komo mai."

There were many more deep lines in the face of Nāihe. He had to be at least ninety years old. His old wife Anuhea had seen them coming with the youngsters, and as she did twenty-seven years ago and probably many times in between, brought out kō, the sugar cane, and offered it to them. The boys loved it and began chewing voraciously, the delicious sweetness flowing down their throats and chins.

'Eleu could hardly breathe, remembering his own past with his friend Keola, chewing on the delicious treat in that very same yard. The children sat in the shade of an old 'ōhi'a 'ai tree, sacred to the Hawaiians with their mother and their new cousin. When the kō was sucked of its juicy sweetness, the boys started on the tasty red fruit of the tall mountain apple tree. 'Eleu approached the porch, and the talk was of pleasantries about the neighborhood, the weather, and the fishing. His wife joined her husband, rocking in tandem with him. He sat at Nāihe's feet and waited, not wanting to be nīele.

The old man studied the young man's face. "I've been waiting for you."

'Eleu was stunned. "You are the son of a man I once knew. Hmmm…what was his name?" He looked to his wife. They looked as if they were separating ancient brain cells one by one to find the right answer. The sentences came in fits and starts.

"I remember a young couple many years ago. Lived up the road. Had a young son."

The old one began to chant in a creaky voice "'A'ohe 'oe e pakele aku, ua lino 'ia i ka lino pāwalu. You won't escape, you are bound with an eight-strand tie…'Eleu is your name. Your father's was Linopāwalu. Anyway, that is what we called him. Your mother…ummmm…Kamahinaohōkū. She died. I remember now.

"The old King Kalani'ōpu'u gave your father a different name. I didn't think it fit him ……Kanewa, but you did not question the king. Your father made beautiful canoes. I am guessing you want to know about your father."

'Eleu was beyond understanding how the old man with dark skin glowing in the summer sun and showing pleasure in the young man with his big smile knew why he was there. 'Eleu was speechless.

Nāihe reached for the tin cup in the barrel and fetched out some water, offering it first to 'Eleu then taking a long drink for himself. It was a bit brackish, another reminder of home.

"King Kalani'ōpu'u was your father's father, your grand-father!" he stated abruptly.

"What?" 'Eleu wanted to scream out loud but knew it rude to interrupt. "I can't believe it." He thought.

The kupuna continued, "At that time he resided at Waiʻōhinu in Kaʻū district and was married to Queen Kānekapōlei, also one of Kamehameha's wives and to other ladies as well.

"There was a servant of his court, a very skilled weaver and a beautiful woman. Her name was Aweolaʻakea translated as Strand of the sacred things of day. She came from Puakalehua, northeast of Waiʻōhinu. Her skill as a weaver of lei niho palaoa, a braided hair lei with whale tooth pendant, was highly sought after by many aliʻi. The king was so infatuated with his servant that he moe (lay) with her. That union produced a child, but to Aweolaʻakea's horror, the king would not accept the keiki, and she was banished from his royal residence and ordered not to tell under penalty of death. She called him Kālei, but his full name was Kalaniikaleiilinopāwalu—The Chief in the Eight Strand Wreath—would be a heavy burden for the rest of his life. The two moved to Hōnaunau to escape their shame. She was your grandmother." Nāihe took a long time before continuing.

"Kalaniʻopuʻu rejected his own son just as I guess your father rejected you." The old man placed his hand on ʻEleu's shoulder. "Yes, I heard reports that you were raised by Kaʻōkaʻi when your mother died. I also heard of your father's exploits in battle, and yours as well. The warriors who came back from the great Oʻahu battle told and retold the story of your father dying in your arms. I see you have twin sons. You know his sons from his wife Kānekapōlei were also twins. Put your mind at rest, ʻEleu. You did not abandon your sons." How could the old man read his thoughts?

"Now…it is my time to leave this place." Breathing heavily, the old man got up and retreated into the hale. Anuhea motioned for them to leave. ʻEleu thanked her profusely, and the little family and their cousin returned to Kalapana without going to Kapaʻahu, his own birthplace.

They stayed a week, 'Eleu trying to decide what to do next. He disliked the thought of subjecting his little family to paddling all the way back home, so he put off the decision for a while.

Kalapana had become larger. He met many relatives who had grown families of their own. The hālau waʻa was still there, enclosing a very large double-hulled canoe. It was used by King Kamehameha when he came to Wahaʻula lua-kini heiau at Kahaualeʻa to offer sacrifice, and any one of his queens and children would swim in the delightful Punaluʻu Pond as part of the sacred complex there.

'Eleu discovered his friend Keola still lived in the area, and he wished to see him again. Kahikina and Ānuenue would remain with Hōkūpaʻa. The two women shared the art of kapa making and were becoming good friends. 'Eleu's wife discovered the delights of the cool Hakuma cave as she and Hōkūpaʻa joined the women occupying themselves with the works of their hands and sharing the gossip of the day.

Kahāipo, the smallest of the twins, wanted to go with his father. 'Eleu picked up his boy and smiled as his arms entwined around his daddy's neck. "My little lei," 'Eleu thought, remembering his mother.

Kapaʻahu was the same. Thatched hale were scattered around the ahupuaʻa. Keola, his wife, and his old father Kaimalino had remained.

Kaimalino cried when he saw 'Eleu. "You look so much like your father. We were best friends, you remember?"

The men caught up with their lives that had been separated by time. Keola and 'Eleu walked up the road toward the old homestead. No one had moved into 'Eleu's hale. The place had disintegrated to a sad state, pili grass rotted back to the ground, supports bent and broken, and everything overgrown by weeds. 'Eleu could hardly contain himself with all the memories.

He buried his head in his son's neck and smelled the fragrance of youth. "I was only a few years younger than you, Kahāipo, when I left home." The boy's arms tightened around his father's neck.

"I want to live here, father."

The hairs on 'Eleu's neck stiffened. "What did you say?"

"I want to live here," he stated emphatically and a little louder. Keola's ears caught the statement.

"But, son, we live in Waimānalo," he said horrified. "That's very far away. What about your mother and your brother?" He wanted to say, "What about me?" but let it die on his lips. "Why?" was the only word to come out of his mouth. A runner interrupted the exchange.

"I have to," the boy whispered in his father's ear.

Annoying 'Eleu no end, the man had a message from Kalapana's head canoe maker. Would 'Eleu come back to the village and go with them on a trip to the forest tomorrow? Shades of a time gone by irritated him, and he wanted to snap the man's head off with an emphatic no but thought better of it. "Yes" came the softer answer. He would have to deal with his son's request later.

Putting his son down, 'Eleu took the boy's hand in his. He bid farewell to Keola, but Keola asked if he could accompany his friend. The three walked on in silence. 'Eleu's mind was swimming. He did not know what to say to Keola, and the silence was uncomfortable. "Why does my boy want to leave his own family and live in Kapaʻahu? What is possessing him to desire such a thing?"

His whole life long, there were aching questions which seemingly had no answers. If he could see far enough in the future, there was usually an explanation or an outcome or choices which guided his life and caused him to be who he was, and he would understand.

In the night, 'Eleu tossed and turned; "The maka pilau again," he thought. Kahikina tossed and turned as well. They woke each other up. "What is wrong, my husband?"

"Keola told me he and his wife are barren," he stated flatly. He sat up. "Let us go outside so we won't wake the boys."

"And what does that have to do with us?" she asked sweetly when they were out in the warm night air under a bright moon.

"Kahāipo wants to stay in Kapa'ahu." She was stunned, and 'Eleu went on. "I do not understand where this is coming from. What are we to do?"

"Have you talked to Keola?"

"Of course not," she thought.

Abruptly, 'Eleu changed the subject. "I was thinking we should go to Hilo and see if we can find a ship to take us home. It's too hard on you and the boys…" his voice trailed off. "I want to go home."

The bud of an idea was coming to Kahikina. "Did Keola talk to him?"

"No. The boy had his arms around my neck the whole time."

"You go in the morning with the men. Let me talk to Kahāipo. Then I will speak with Keola and his wife."

Kahāipo told his mother simply that Kaimalino would be gone soon and "There will be no one to take care of them in their old age. Their house is cold without the love of a child."

Kahikina was astonished with her child's wisdom. "Where did it come from? Maybe these are signs of being a kāula, a seer…" she wondered.

The men were gone only a few days as the hō'ailona, the portents, were bad. A stormy wind came on them suddenly as they made their way on the volcano trail above the Hōlei Pali. 'Elepaio birds seemed to be busier than usual among the forest trees pecking at the trunks. Even the goddess Pele seemed to be displeased as a cloud of smoke rose from the distant Kīlauea volcano. The party turned around before disaster overtook them.

There were wrinkles in ʻEleu's brow when he returned. He vacillated between the love of his son and love for his friend. Back and forth, he argued with himself. But in the end, his ʻaumākua gave him the answer he needed. Hānai was the Hawaiian form of adoption, a way of being kind and generous to those family or friends who were childless. He and Kahikina were blessed to have two boys, and for some reason, Kahāipo knew it was the right thing to do. But he also knew that he must live in Kapaʻahu. That stumped ʻEleu.

Kahikina noticed her husband's worried face and pulled him aside. "Let us walk to Kapaʻahu, ʻEleu."

Clouds darkened the sky and ʻEleu wondered if it were wise to walk anywhere. He hesitated. She took his hand, and he gave no protest.

"I spoke with Kahāipo. Our son does not know where his desire comes from but knows it is right. When he was very little, he was so different from Ānuenue, who was always running and playing. Kahāipo was the thoughtful one, always contented to sit and watch the sky, observing the way the wind blew and the clouds moved, and listening to the sound of the sea. He was always vigilant. He seemed to know when I needed comfort and when I would lose courage that you would ever return to us. I suspect there is something in him that needs to be fulfilled. He is extremely sensitive to the grief of Keola and his wife. We will walk to their home."

Continuing on in silence, ʻEleu felt the connection of their hands as if there was a strand that ran between them, and just then, the words of Waiʻaha's wife came back to him, "You are a kahuna kilokilo. Use it well." It was an expert who observed the skies for omens. Was this his son's destiny?

Keola's home was on the ma uka side of the trail across from the canoe-launching ladder at Kī. The friends greeted each other warmly, but 'Eleu felt a sense of doom. The clouds were darker as they settled themselves under a tree. The couple only had a sleeping hale divided in two rooms, one for Kaimalino and the other for Keola and his wife. There was also a hale pe'a for his wife's kapu time. It seemed a poor place with only an imu out of doors and some potato patches. The care for the elderly father was time consuming, and they were only able to eke out the bare minimum of vegetable food to trade for fish. 'Eleu felt deep sorrow for the couple, and it was dawning on him just what was making his son feel for them.

"Hilahila loa. We feel ashamed of our barrenness," the wife, whose name was Pua'ala, explained with tears in her eyes. They had been married for ten years and still had no keiki.

'Eleu's homestead was just a short distance away on the ma kai side of the trail. There were fish ponds and a line of coconut trees along the trail to the mountain. Kanewa had built all the proper dwellings for their family with room to spare for visitors. It only took a moment for him to see what must be done.

They came to an agreement. Kahāipo would stay with his hanai parents and be their child. The homestead in Kapa'ahu would be rebuilt with the help of the neighbors, and 'Eleu would leave his father's canoe for the boy to help his new parents. Suddenly, the clouds were blown away by a ho'olua wind from the mountain to the ocean, and the sea was calm, and the doom that had befallen the little family was gone. In the weeks ahead, Kaimalino died in the arms of his new grandson.

There seemed to be a great weight lifted off the shoulders of everyone, and while the parting would be sad for

'Eleu's family, there was also happiness that everything was pono, right.

When they arrived back at Kalapana, an unknown canoe was in the little bay, and a man was talking to the konohiki. 'Eleu found his aunt Hōkūpa'a with the crowd that had gathered around.

"King Kamehameha wants the 'iliahi we have collected," she related. "Come, let me introduce you. This could be an answer to your prayers."

The konohiki had been up the mountain with the men for many months, cutting down the beautiful 'iliahi, the coveted sandalwood with the fragrant heart used by the Hawaiians to give a pleasant aroma to their kapa garments and bedding. The sandalwood tree was beginning to be used for trade purposes and shipped from O'ahu to Canton, China, where it was consumed as highly desirable incense.

The messenger had heard of 'Eleu and was glad to meet him. They walked to the canoe shed. "I hear you need a ride to Waimānalo," he said while the konohiki removed the covers of woven lauhala mats.

What 'Eleu had thought was a double-hulled canoe was actually a peleleu war canoe that had been built at Kealakekua. "Was it one that I had worked on?" he wondered. And behind the shed was a huge pile of 'iliahi ready to be loaded.

"They want it immediately on O'ahu," the man told him. "If you paddle, I'll take you and your family to Kākuhihewa?"

That was good news to 'Eleu, and he was more than happy to help.

It took the entire village to move the canoe off the huge carved stands of milo wood onto the smooth hau log rollers and gingerly take it down to the sea. They anchored and tied it securely. Then the long line of men moved the 'iliahi logs hand-over-hand to the waiting platform from which the cover and the sails had been removed. It took many hours to accomplish the task and tie the load securely. 'Eleu, with his expertise at lashing, was pleased to be doing the work. The logs ranged in length from seven to twenty-five feet.

All was ready to go. There were forty paddlers, twenty on either side including 'Olu'olu. Kahikina and Ānuenue were in the bow. Everyone else had gathered on the beach to say good-bye and to send good wishes and prayers for their safe journey. One thing left for 'Eleu to do was to make the sacrifice of a pig for the canoe and the journey it was about to undertake. He slit its throat, and the village kahuna offered it to the gods.

Keola had come down to Kalapana with his new son in his arms. It was a tearful parting. The twin brothers hugged and cried, and Ānuenue would not be consoled. Kahikina took her beloved son Kahāipo in her arms and told him how much she loved him and to follow the path he had chosen. 'Eleu's heart was breaking. He knelt on the ground in front of the boy, and the two looked into each other's eyes for a long while as if to memorize their faces. They hugged and touched noses, giving and taking from each other the hā, the breath of life. There were no words exchanged; there could be none, only the love shared between a father and his son.

'Eleu had never paddled the peleleu canoes. They were huge and heavy and rode the waves amazingly well especially with the heavy load. Would it be ungainly on the open sea? Would it survive the tortuous 'Alenuihāhā Channel between Hawai'i Island and Maui? Always, the questions, but all would reveal itself in the coming days on the way home. 'Eleu smiled broadly with wind and sea spray in his face. The paddle went in the water, and he pulled mightily, using the 'ūlili, the flooring on which the paddlers stood in the six-foot deep hulls, and he felt the big schooner-like canoe beneath him. He had turned his face to the little bay at Kalapana with a twinge of sorrow and glimpsed his son waving good-bye, but his great-grandfather, Kaʻōkaʻi, just as he had done so many times before turned ʻEleu's head to the future.

The oli ʻEleu chanted with his deep full-vibratoed voice was a prayer to the goddess Lea and the god Kū. The chant encouraged the men. They heard. They sang. They paddled, rejoicing. All on shore listened until they could hear no more, but those who knew continued the chant together along the beautiful black-sand beach.

EPILOGUE

Waimānalo, Oʻahu—the Present Day
(One Week Later)

The reunion week on Hawaiʻi Island was over, and Keoki drove the immediate family home from Honolulu Airport. Within five miles, all the passengers were asleep. Liana and Keoki quietly talked in the front seat of the SUV about the success of the event, the renewal of old acquaintances, and the connection with new ʻohana. The best news of all was the recording of the amazing historical strands of ancestry. Liana and Leona would collaborate in writing down all the stories and the points of view of the oldest surviving members of the family. It would be published for the moʻopuna, the grandchildren, and generations to come. They were satisfied that the results of the reunion had been accomplished.

Papa was exhausted after the trip home and was completely drained after all the reminiscences and the final disclosure of the eight-strand lei of his ancestors' history to his family. After a few days, Tūtū Kanani was worried that her husband wasn't responding to the rest he needed and insisted he go to the doctor. He just shrugged and said he'd be all right. In the late afternoon, she called Keoki, suggesting they go for an early dinner at a favorite spot in Kailua.

"Maybe that will perk him up a little," she said hopefully.

Keoki noticed that his grandfather didn't have much of an appetite until his favorite dessert came, apple pie à la mode. He enjoyed the treat so much. Keoki drove them home to Waimānalo, and Tūtū Kanani had them stay for some coffee. The children went off to play, and the women sat in the living room watching the evening news.

Granddad wanted to sit on the lanai with Keoki. The evening was beautiful. They made small talk while drinking their coffee and watching the night come in across the sea.

"That apple pie...It was real 'ono! Second to none! Keoki,...I want to tell you something..." He took the last sip of his coffee, enjoying it immensely. "You know...everyone calls me Albert..." his voice was just above a whisper as he gazed at the ocean.

"Yes, Papa, I know." Keoki was alarmed by his grandfather's sudden shortness of breath.

Barely above a whisper, "My...Hawaiian name is...'Eleu."

Keoki grasped the cup as it slid off his Granddad's lap. Just as he did that, the father, the grandfather, the great-grandfather closed his eyes on the last gold rays of the sun stretching across the sky west of the mountains. The clouds reflected their warm hues bathing the glorious 'āina from the Ko'olau Mountains to the sea. The sunset was staggering in its brilliant beauty. The mountain's green summits were wreathed in coral and gray lei po'o. But dark recesses like thieves began snatching away the land. Bands of clouds pressed on by breezes stretched across the sky and changed from coral to gray then disappeared. Water and sky in color of kai uli, the deep blue sea, disappeared. After a lifetime of hard work, Papa's heart stopped. His 'uhane left him there on that porch in his family home in Waimānalo with Keoki by his side. The canoe maker's son paddled off into the darkness, the strand to be passed to a new generation.

A woman's voice was heard off in the distance, melodiously calling her son's inoa kāhea: "'Eleu...'Eleu...'Eleu wawā kini kini...'Eleu wawā kini kini ka noho 'ana kau hale mehameha..."

THE END

GLOSSARY OF HAWAIIAN WORDS

A

'aha: Cord braided of coconut husk.

ahu lā'ī: Ti-leaf raincoat or cape.

ahupua'a: Land divisions within districts sometimes extending from inland to the sea.

'āina: Land.

'ākia: Endemic shrubs and trees (Wikstroemia).

aloha kākou: May there be friendship or love between us; greetings to more than one.

aloha kāua: May there be friendship or love between us; greetings to one person.

ama: Outrigger float.

Ānuenue: Rainbow.

'awapuhi: Wild ginger.

'awa: kava *(Piper methysticum)* A shrub.

Aweola'akea [Awe-o-La'a-Kea]: Strand of sacred things of day: sunshine, knowledge, happiness.

E

'elepaio: A species of flycatcher.

'Eleu: Active, alert, energetic, ambitious.

'Eleu wawā kini kini ka noho 'ana kau hale mehameha: The lonely but ambitious warrior who went from village to village. Everyone he goes to, the villagers bring gifts to his feet.

H

ha'ina 'ia mai ana ka puana: Tell the summary refrain (tell the story in the refrain).

hala: Pandanus or screw pine; see also lauhala.

hālau: Long house for hula instruction.

hālau wa'a: Long house for canoe.

hale: House.

hale moe: Sleeping house.

hale mua: Men's eating house.

hao: The pre-contact word for iron.

hau: A lowland tree (Hibiscus tiliaceus).

hoa pili: Close, intimate, personal friend.

hoka: Disappointed; thwarted; baffled.

holomū: A long fitted dress; a combination of holokū and mu'umu'u.

honi: To kiss; formerly to touch the side of the nose.

ho'opupule: To make insane, to drive crazy

huewai: Water gourd.

I

i'a: Fish or any marine animal.

'iako: Outrigger boom.

'iliahi: Sandalwood.

imu: Underground oven
'inamona: A mashed relish made with cooked kernel of kukui and salt.
inoa kāhea: Calling name.
ipu: Bottle gourd
ipu heke 'ole: Without a top.

K

Kahāipo: The sweetheart's breath.
kahuna: Expert of secret or sacred knowledge.
kahuna kālai wa'a: Expert canoe builder.
kahuna lā'au lapa'au: Curing expert (medical practitioner).
kahuna kilokilo: Expert who observes the skies for omens.
Kaimalino: Calm sea.
kalo: Taro; staple food from earliest times; all parts of the plant are eaten especially the corm (root) from which poi is made, and the lū'au (leaves).
kama'āina: Land child, native born.
Kamuela: Samuel.
Kanani: The beauty.
kani ka pila: Play music.
kapa: Cloth made from the wauke tree.
kapu: Taboo.
kaula: Rope; cord; string.
kauā (or kauwā): Servant or slave.
keiki 'alu'alu: Premature baby.
Ka'ōka'i: The tendrils of a plant; to grow, interlock, interweave as tendrils.
Keoki: George.
Keola: The life.
kī hō'alu: Slack key, the first and last strings of the guitar are tuned to D instead of E.
kanaka: Human being; man; person; Hawaiian.

kānaka: Plural form of kanaka.

kāne: Man or men.

kīhei: Cape

kīpuka: Holes (spaces) of green vegetation between lava flows.

koa: Warrior; acacia koa tree.

Kū: The ancient god of war.

kūkae: Excreta; filth.

kukui: Candlenut tree (*Aleurites moluccana*).

kupuna: Grandparent; ancestor; relative.

L

lauhala: Leaves of the (see) hala.

laua'e: A fragrant fern.

lei: A neck wreath; figuratively, a child or loved one of one's own generation.

lei niho palaoa: Braided hair lei with sperm whale tooth ornament.

lei po'o: Head lei.

limu: Edible seaweed.

Lino: To weave, twist, braid or tie.

lo'i: Irrigated terrace for growing kalo.

lua: General name for a type of hand-to-hand fighting.

luakini: Type of heiau where the ruling chief's offered human sacrifices.

lū'au: Young taro tops; Hawaiian feast.

M

māhoe: Twins.

maile: A native twining shrub.

ma kai: Toward the sea.

maka'āinana: Commoner; people of the land.

maka piapia: Eyes sticky with viscous matter.
malo: Male's loincloth.
manu: Bird; upper decorative end pieces of bow and stern.
ma uka: Toward the mountain.
moku: Island; Ship, said to be so called because the first European ships suggested islands.
moʻo: Gunnel strakes—side planks fitted to the middle section on each side of a canoe hull.
moʻokūʻauhau: Genealogy.

N

nīele: Inquisitive; rude.
nohona waʻa: Seat.
Nootka Tribe: Present day Nuu-chah-nulth (all along the mountains).

O

ʻohana: Family.
ʻōhiʻa lehua: (*metrosideros macropus*).
ʻōhiʻa ʻai: Mountain apple tree *(Eugenia malaccensis)*.
ʻōkole: Buttocks.
ʻōlelo maoli: Hawaiian language.
ʻōlepe: Oysters, mussels, and clams.
oli: Chant.
ʻolowai: Canoe water gourd.
ʻOluʻolu: Pleasant; nice.
ʻomo: Calabash bowl covers.
ʻono: Delicious.
ʻŌnohi: Fragment of a rainbow.
ʻopihi: Limpets.
ʻōpū: Belly; stomach; abdomen.

P

paepae wa'a: Canoe ladder.
pahu hula: Hula drum.
Papa: A pet name for a grandfather or great-grandfather.
Pāwa'a: One of King Kamehameha's navy yards (now near intersection of Kalakaua Ave. and S. King St.). It was a lagoon.
pepeiao: Comb cleats for canoe seats.
pīkoi: A tripping club with rope attached.
pilau: Stench; *ho'o pilau*: Cause a stench.
pili: A grass used for thatch.
po'e: People.
pū: Coil of hair; topknot.
Pualani Ki'eki'e: Heavenly flower; high, tall, and lofty.

S

Strait of Juan de Fuca: ha·č?iq tupał (pronounced hahts'-i<u>k</u> too-puhlth) It means 'the long salt water (ocean)'— in the language of the Makah, Olympic Peninsula, Washington State

T

taro: See kalo.
Tūtū (also Kūkū): Grandmother or grandfather.

U

'uhane: Spirit.
'uku: Flea.
'ūlili: Subflooring in deep-hulled canoes.
'ulu: Breadfruit.

'upena ku'u: Gill net.
'upena 'ulu'ulu: The old term for throw nets.

W

wa'a: Canoe.
wae: U-shaped canoe spreaders.
Waimānalo: Potable water.
wauke: Paper mulberry tree; shrub from which kapa is made.

Author's own photograph of a Hawaiian
canoe paddler petroglyph.

SELECTED BIBLIOGRAPHY

Abbott, Isabella Aiona. *Lāʻau Hawaiʻi*: Traditional Hawaiian Uses of Plants. Honolulu: Bishop Museum Press, 1992.

Barman, Jean, and Bruce McIntyre Watson. *Leaving Paradise: Indigenous Hawaiians in the Pacific Northwest 1787-1898*. University of Hawaii Press, June 1, 2006.

Barrow, Terrence. *Captain Cook in Hawaiʻi*: Norfolk Island, Australia: Island Heritage, 1976.

Bird, Adren J. and Steven Goldsberry, and J. Puninani Kanekoa Bird. *The Craft of Hawaiian Lauhala Weaving*: University of Hawaii Press, 1982.

Chickering, William H. *Within the Sound of These Waves: The Story of Old Hawaii,* 1st ed. Harcourt, Brace and Company, 1941.

Cordy, Ross. *The Rise and Fall of the Oʻahu Kingdom*. Mutual Publishing, October 1, 2002.

Cordy, Ross. *Exalted Sits the Chief.* Mutual Publishing, 2000.

Daws, Gavan. *Shoal of Time: A History of the Hawaiian Islands.* New York: MacMillan, 1968.

de Freycinet, Louis Claude de Saulses. *Hawaiʻi in 1819: A Narrative Account by Louis Claude de Saulses de Freycinet.* Translated by Ella L. Wiswell. Edited by Marion

Kelly. Number 26–Pacific Anthropological Records. Bishop Museum.

Desha, Stephen Langhern. *Kamehameha and His Warrior Kekūhaupiʻo.* Translated by Frances N. Frazier. Honolulu: Kamehameha Schools Press, 2000.

DeVoto, Bernard, Editor and Interpreted. *The Journals of Lewis and Clark.* Sentry Edition, (Massachussetts: The Riverside Press Cambridge, 1963).

Ellis, William. *A Narrative of an 1823 Tour Through Hawaii: Journal of William Ellis.* Mutual Publishing, 2004.

Feher, Joseph. *Hawaiʻi: A Pictorial.* Bishop Museum Press, 1969.

Giesecke, E. W. *Discovery of Humboldt Bay, California, in 1806 from the Ship O'Cain, Jonathan Winship, Commander: An Episode in a Bostonian-Russian Contract Voyage of the Early American China Trade.* PDF

Fort Ross Conservancy (FRC) asks that you acknowledge FRC as the distributor of the content; if you use material from FRC's online library, we request that you link directly to the URL provided. If you use the content offline, we ask that you credit the source as follows: "Digital content courtesy of Fort Ross Conservancy, www.fortross.org; author maintains copyright of his or her written material."

Handy, Edward Smith Craighill, and Elizabeth Green Handy. *Native Planters in Old Hawaiʻi: Their Life, Lore, and Environment,* rev. ed. With Mary Kawena Pukui. Bernice P. Bishop Museum Bulletin, 233. Honolulu: Bishop Museum Press, 1991.

Holmes, Tommy. *The Hawaiian Canoe,* Editions Limited, 1996.

Hopkins, Jerry. *How to Make Your Own Hawaiian Musical Instruments.* Bess Press, 1988.

Howay, Judge F. W. *Forty-Second Annual Report of the Hawaiian Historical Society for the Year 1933 (The Ship Eliza at Hawai'i in 1799)* May, 1934, 103.

Howe, K.R., editor. *Vaka Moana* Voyages of the Ancestors, The Discovery and Settlement of the Pacific: University of Hawai'i Press, 2007.

Kamehameha Schools Press. *Life in Early Hawai'i, The Ahupua'a.* Kamehameha Schools Press, 1994.

Kāne, Herb Kawainui. *Voyagers.* Edited by Paul Berry. Bellevue, WA: Whale Song, 1991.

Kāne, Herb Kawainui. *Ancient Hawai'i.* Captain Cook, HI: Kawainui Press, 1997.

Kauhi, Emma Kapūnohu'ulaokalani. *He Mo'olelo no Kapa'ahu.* Hilo: Pili Productions, 1996.

Olson, Ronald L. *Adze, Canoe, and House Types of the Northwest Coast.* University of Washington Press, Seattle, Washington, 1927

Paglinawan, Richard Kekumuikawaiokeola, and Eli Mitchell, and Moses Elwood Kalauokalni, and Jerry Walker. *Lua: Art of the Hawaiian Warrior.* Bishop Museum, 2006.

Pukui, Mary Kawena, and Haertig, E. W., and Catherine A. Lee. *Nānā I Ke Kumu Vol. I and Vol, II: Look to the Source.* Hui Hānai, An Auxiliary of the Queen Lili'uokalani Children's Center, Honolulu HI, September 11, 2014.

Stewart, Hilary. Annotated and Illustrated. *The Adventures and Sufferings of John R. Jewitt, Captive of Chief Maquinna* – Jewitt's Narrative. Douglas & McIntyre, 1987; first paperback printing, 1995.

Sturgis, William, and S.W. Jackman, Editor. ** *The Journal of William Sturgis.* Sono Nis Press, 1978.

Watterman, T. T. *The Whaling Equipment of the Makah Indians.* Seattle, Wash. University of Washington Publications in Political and Social Science, June, 1920.

Yenne, Bill, and Susan Garratt. *North American Indians.* Ottenheimer Publishers Inc., 1994.

    * Barrow: This is where the story comes from about Bligh saving the canoe with the old man, younger man, and a six-year-old under the thwart.

    ** Sturgis: My ship the *Marguerite Ann* is based on the ship *Eliza,* and Captain Rowan's journal.

PRONUNCIATION GUIDE

The Hawaiian Alphabet

Vowels:
a (ah), e (eh), i (ee), o (oh), u (oooh)

Consonants:
h, k, l, m, n, p, w

Other:
' ('okina = glottal stop, used in between vowels to break up or separate its sound)
- (kahakō = macron, used above vowels to elongate its sound)

Names

'Eleu wawā kinikini ka noho 'ana kau hale mehameha
'eh-le-ooh-vah-vaah-key-nee-key-nee-kah-noh-ho-'ah-nuhkah-ooh-hah-leh-meh-uh-meh-huh

Hikuokalani
hee-koo-oh-kah-lah-nee

Huapala
hoo-ah-pah-luh

Kanewa
Kah-neh-vuh

Keola
keh-oh-luh

Kaimalino
kah-ee-mah-lee-noh

Nāihe
nuh-ee-heh

Kamahinaohōkū
kah-mah-heen-hah-oh-hoh-koo

Ka'ōka'i
ka-'oh-kah-'ee

Hōkūpa'a
hoh-koo-pah-'uh

Wai'aha
why-'ah-huh

Kealakōwa'a
keh-ah-lah-koh-vah-'uh

Kuluwaimaka
koo-loo-vah-ee-mah-kuh

Waha'ula
vah-hah-'ooh-luh

La'imi
lah-'ee-mee

Ahipu'u
ah-hee-pooh-'ooh

Kalanikupule
kah-lah-nee-koo-pooh-leh

Kahikina
kah-hee-key-nuh

Pā'ū o Lu'ukia
pah-'ooh-oh-loo-'ooh-key-uh

Kahāipo
kah-hah-ee-poh

Kanēkapolei
kah-neh-kah-poh-leh-ee

Aweola'akea
ah-veh-oh-lah-'ah-keh-uh

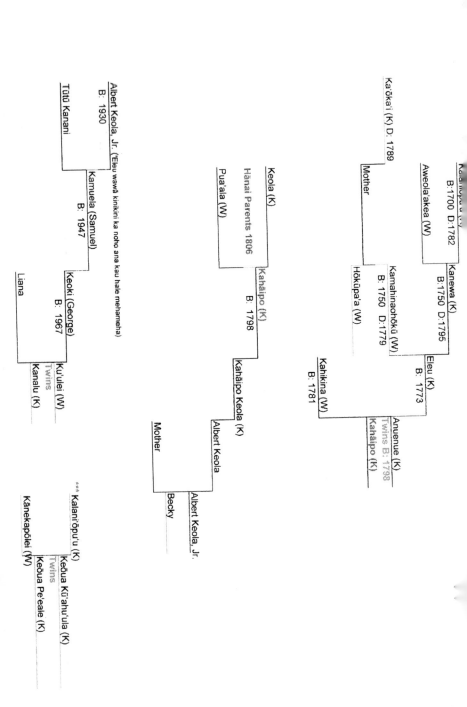

Kaōkaʻi (K) D: 1789

Kalaniōpuʻu (K)

Kanewa (K)
B:1700 D:1782

Aweola'iakea (W)

Kanewa (K)
B:1750 D:1795

Mother

Kamahinaohōkū (W)
B: 1750 D:1779

Eleu (K)
B: 1773

Hōkūpaʻa (W)

Kahikina (W)
B: 1781

Anuenue (K)
Twins B: 1798
Kahāipo (K)

Keola (K)

Puaʻala (W)

Hānai Parents 1806

Kahāipo (K)
B: 1798

Kahāipo Keola (K)

Albert Keola

Mother

Albert Keola, Jr.

Becky

Albert Keola, Jr. (ʻEleu wawā kinikini ka noho ana kau hale mehameha)
B: 1930

Tūtū Kanani

Kamuela (Samuel)
B: 1947

Liana

Keoki (George)
B: 1967

Ku'ulei (W)
Twins
Kanalu (K)

*** Kalaniʻōpuʻu (K)

Keōua Kūʻahuʻula (K)
Twins
Keōua Pe'eale (K)

Kānekapōlei (W)

ABOUT THE ARTIST

Brook Kapūkuniahi Parker is a Native Hawaiian artist from Kahaluʻu, Oʻahu. His artwork reflects ancestral ties to Hawaiian warriors and aliʻi, including Kamehameha the Great and his wife Kanekapolei. An accomplished illustrator and public speaker, Brook's recent work includes commissions from the University of Hawaiʻi and the Aulani Disney Resort.

ABOUT THE AUTHOR

After the death of her husband Charles Kanewa in Los Angeles in 2003, Cecilia met his cousin a year later at a Hawai'i Marines Reunion in Las Vegas. She fell in love with the handsome virile cowboy and after four months, she took a leap of faith and moved to Hawai'i to marry Bernard Johansen and live in the lush up-country of Waimea on Hawai'i Island. They were only married for five years before his untimely death. Stories from the lives of the two cousins growing up in Kapa'ahu, Puna District, and extensive research have led to her first novel *The Canoe Maker's Son*.

Cecilia is a new writer and has published stories and poetry in *North Hawaii News*, *Freida* Magazine, and contributed her husbands' stories to *Hali'a Aloha no Kalapana* (Fond Memories of Kalapana), a project sponsored by the Hawai'i Council for the Humanities and the Teresa Lee Waipa Trust. She is contemplating to write another novel about the beautiful Hawaiian people and their history, and she continues to live in Waimea, enjoying the rainy coolness of the pastures and her dog Maka Polu.

CPSIA information can be obtained at www.ICGtesting.com
Printed in the USA
LVOW11s1009270916

506378LV00001B/11/P